"Hold on. You don't want to knock that bandage loose."

He walked over, stretched the neck of the sweatshirt and helped slip it over her head. Her soft hair slid over his f... satin brushing his skin.

Their eyes ... k-boxed in his sk... aware of how ... arm, lush lips were j... his.

He need... step away. He couldn't succumb t... urge to kiss Zoe. But everything inside him clamored to touch her, feel her, taste her again….

He should let her go. This was the wrong place, the wrong time. Zoe was off-limits, part of his surveillance case. *Taboo.*

But he never had obeyed the rules.

Dear Reader,

Superheroes have never impressed me much. I prefer reading—and writing—about ordinary people who get caught in extraordinary circumstances, people who have to use their wits to survive.

Scientist Zoe Wilkinson is one such person. Her quiet world explodes when her grandfather is kidnapped and she finds herself under suspicion for espionage. Desperately out of her comfort zone, pursued by everyone from government agents to deadly gunmen, Zoe must scramble just to stay alive. And when she gets stranded in the desert with her ex-lover Cooper Kennedy, a sexy pilot with an agenda of his own, she faces danger of a different sort.

I had a great time watching Zoe and Coop unravel this puzzling case—and battle the sizzling attraction that won't subside. I hope you enjoy their race through the desert heat!

Gail Barrett

GAIL BARRETT

Meltdown

ROMANTIC
SUSPENSE

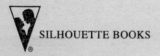

SILHOUETTE BOOKS

ISBN-13: 978-0-373-27680-6

MELTDOWN

Recycling programs
for this product may
not exist in your area.

This edition published by arrangement with Harlequin Books S.A.

For questions and comments about the quality of this book please contact us at Customer_eCare@Harlequin.ca.

® and TM are trademarks of Harlequin Books S.A., used under license. Trademarks indicated with ® are registered in the United States Patent and Trademark Office, the Canadian Trade Marks Office and in other countries.

Visit Silhouette Books at www.eHarlequin.com

Printed in U.S.A.

Books by Gail Barrett

Silhouette Romantic Suspense

Facing the Fire #1414
★*Heart of a Thief* #1514
★*To Protect a Princess* #1538
His 7-Day Fiancée #1560
★*The Royal Affair* #1601
Meltdown #1610

Silhouette Special Edition

Where He Belongs #1722

★The Crusaders

GAIL BARRETT

Gail Barrett always knew she'd be a writer. Who else would spend her childhood grinding sparkling rocks into fairy dust and convincing her friends it was real? Or daydream her way through elementary school, spend high school reading philosophy and playing the bagpipes, and then head off to Spain during college to live the writer's life? After four years she straggled back home—broke, but fluent in Spanish. She became a teacher, earned a master's degree in linguistics, married a Coast Guard officer and had two sons.

But she never lost the desire to write. Then one day, she discovered a Silhouette Intimate Moments novel in a bookstore—and knew she was destined to write romance. Her books have won numerous awards, including a National Readers' Choice Award and Romance Writers of America's prestigious Golden Heart.

She currently lives in western Maryland. Readers can contact her through her Web site, www.gailbarrett.com.

To my wonderful agent, Pam Hopkins, for her support over all these years.

Acknowledgments

I'd like to thank the following people for their enormous help with this book: Eber Crossley, Bob Mills and Piper Rome for answering my aviation questions; Chris Sarno for being a good sport and letting me sit in his plane; Robin Farley for providing military details; Mike Morrell, Rich Talipsky and Maggie Toussaint for inventing a brilliant nuclear process; John K. Barrett for teaching me how to shoot; and Joe Barrett, for patiently explaining computer encryption. These extremely competent people tried their best to help me, and I take full responsibility for any and all mistakes.

Chapter 1

She'd stumbled into a nightmare.

Zoe Wilkinson clutched the steering wheel of her rattling Honda, her fingers numb, her breath coming in labored gasps, her gaze locked on the remote Nevada airstrip shimmering ahead in the desert haze. Her calm, orderly existence had exploded. The tranquillity she'd sought her entire life had been torn into shreds.

She jerked her gaze from the bumpy dirt road and braved a glance in her rearview mirror. Dust billowed behind her speeding car, obscuring her view of the black sedan. But those killers were back there, following her. They'd broken into her apartment, chased her through the mountains outside of Ely, pursued her into the wide-open desert where she couldn't hide.

She sucked in a reedy breath and slammed the gas pedal flat to the floor. "Come on," she pleaded to the car. "Go faster." She had to make it to the tiny airstrip and beg a flight to the ghost town where her grandfather had hidden that flash drive.

Before both she and her grandfather died.

Raw hysteria burbled inside her. She tried to swallow, but her throat was dustier than the sand stretching to the horizon on every side.

This shouldn't be happening. She was a nuclear chemist. She'd led a staid, quiet life for years. She shouldn't have the FBI monitoring her movements, rumors of espionage swirling around her, unknown assailants dogging her heels.

And her grandfather—a world-renowned physicist— kidnapped, suspected of treason.

Possibly dead.

Terror slashed her belly at that dreadful thought, but she forced the fear aside. He couldn't die. She wouldn't let him. He was the only family she had left. And no way was he a traitor, no matter what the FBI claimed. He would never sell nuclear secrets to enemy agents. This was all a horrific mistake.

The Honda jolted into a rut, snapping her head back against the headrest, and she nearly lost control of the car. She clenched her teeth, tightened her fingers on the vibrating wheel, her biceps and shoulders aching from the battle to stay on the road. But she didn't dare slow. Her pursuers had nearly caught up.

She had no clue who those men were. FBI? CIA? *The kidnappers?* They'd barged into her apartment wielding weapons, black hoods covering their heads. It was a miracle she'd escaped.

And she wasn't out of danger yet.

She squinted out the insect-splattered windshield at the airstrip a quarter mile away now—its listing, sun-bleached flight shack, the two geriatric Cessnas parked on the dirt runway, the peeling Winnebago squatting amidst the sagebrush like a decaying bug.

She frantically scanned the airstrip for Pedro, the reclusive old pilot who owned the place, but didn't see him around. He *had* to be there. He had to fly her to that ghost town. He was her only hope.

Keeping the accelerator flattened to the floorboard, she hurtled the final few yards to the airstrip, sparing another glance behind her at the swarms of dust. Too panicked to slow, she yanked on the wheel, swerved toward the airstrip's entrance.

But the car hit another rut, knocking her hands loose. She lunged for the wheel but couldn't regain control. The car careened through the sagebrush and smashed through the split rail fence. She shrieked, flinched, as the wooden rails crashed apart and bounced off the hood.

She twisted hard on the wheel and slammed on the brakes, her heart going berserk. The car fishtailed in the sand, flinging her against the door, then jerked to a stop in a spray of dust.

Shaking violently, she gasped for breath. Still panting, she pried her fingers off the steering wheel and pressed her hand to her aching head. But she'd worry about her bruises later. She had to get out of here—fast.

She cut the engine, and the abrupt silence echoed in her ears. Moving quickly, she grabbed her knapsack from the passenger seat, shoved open her door, then stumbled out onto the sand. The dust drifted, then began to settle. She tossed her blond braid over her shoulder and lifted her hand to shield her eyes from the blazing sun.

Tumbleweeds rolled past the trailer. Insects buzzed with a vengeance nearby. The wind sock on the flight shack made a halfhearted flutter in the scorching breeze, but nothing else moved. There was no other sound. No sign of Pedro.

But the nearest plane had its cockpit door open, so he had to be around.

"Pedro?" she called out, starting toward the two planes sitting on the runway behind the flight shack. "Are you there?"

No one answered. She cast a worried glance at the road, spotted the dust cloud about two miles back.

"Pedro?" she called again, her anxiety rising. She whirled around, skimmed her gaze over the sagebrush and cactus flanking the trailer, the iron water pump jutting out of the sand.

Still nothing. The airstrip appeared deserted.

Dragging air into her strangled lungs, she tried to quell the panic ballooning inside. She couldn't fail her grandfather, not after she'd already messed up so badly. She should have paid more attention to his erratic behavior, should have believed his claims earlier that someone was spying on him. Instead, she'd shrugged off his paranoid ramblings as the delusions of an aging man.

And now, as a result, he could die.

A movement in her peripheral vision caught her attention, and she whipped around. A man strode toward her from the runway—but he was too tall, his hair too dark to be Pedro's.

Her pulse sped up. Her hands trembling, she dug in her knapsack for her can of Mace. The man rounded the flight shack, heading straight toward her, a greasy rag balled in his fist.

He lifted his head. His gaze collided with hers. He came to a sudden stop.

And her world tilted even more.

"Coop?" she whispered, a sudden wave of dizziness

blurring her eyes. It couldn't be him. Talk about a nightmare.

But she couldn't mistake the man she'd once loved—even after eight long years. His thick, blue-black hair gleamed in the sunshine. The faint shadow of black stubble darkened his bronzed jaw. Her gaze traced the jut of his noble nose, the slant of his high cheekbones—evidence of an Apache ancestor in the family tree.

Cooper Kennedy. The man she'd adored. The man who'd dumped her. The man who'd haunted her dreams for years.

She closed her eyes, then snapped them open again—but he wasn't a mirage. Coop closed the distance between them, his big body bristling with anger, his stony gaze clamped on hers.

He was taller now, his shoulders broader under his navy-blue T-shirt, more muscled than that last, dreadful time that they'd met. And his once-shaggy hair was shorter, thanks to his Naval Aviator career. Laugh lines creased the corners of his eyes.

But he wasn't laughing now.

Her gaze dropped to his mouth—that wickedly sensual mouth that had launched her to paradise—then back to his slate-gray eyes.

He looked less wild, more controlled.

More dangerous.

Angry as hell.

And she absolutely did not need this. Her life had turned disastrous enough.

She stepped back, started to turn away to hunt for Pedro, but he intercepted the move and blocked her flight. "What the *hell* were you trying to do, kill yourself?" His deep voice vibrated with fury. His flinty eyes bored into hers. "You almost hit the trailer."

"I…" She shook her head, still dazed at his appearance, unwilling to take time to explain. She shot a glance at the road, caught sight of the black sedan speeding closer to the airstrip, unable to stifle a flurry of dread. "Where's Pedro?"

"Gone."

"Gone?" She snapped her gaze back to Coop's. "Gone where?"

"He's on vacation."

"Vacation?" She gaped at him, staggered by the thought. "But…that's ridiculous. Impossible." Pedro never left the desert. He rarely even ventured into nearby Big Rock—population 53—unless he needed tequila or beans.

Coop folded his arms over his broad chest, his eyes turning colder yet. "He's visiting a niece in Colorado."

"Colorado." She gave her head a quick shake, but it still didn't make any sense. Pedro had never mentioned a niece, and he never left the airstrip. He'd flown her grandfather to that ghost town like clockwork every few weeks for years.

And why on earth was Coop here? He was supposed to be living his dream, flying a fighter jet somewhere. She'd never imagined he'd return to the same hard-scrabble patch of sand he'd spent his life trying to escape.

But none of that mattered right now. She flicked her gaze back to the road, and a fresh jolt of anxiety clawed through her nerves. The sedan was less than a mile away. *She had to go.*

She met Coop's unyielding eyes, struggling to keep the strain from her voice. "Look, I need a ride. Right now. To Crater Canyon."

"The planes are grounded."

"They can't be." Her voice rose. "I need a flight."

"Tough." He turned and strode in the direction of the

trailer, and her desperation surged. He had to help her. She couldn't drive to the ghost town—she'd never outrun that sedan.

"Coop, wait," she called to his retreating back. "Please. You have to help me."

He stopped, slowly pivoted to face her, his eyes so furious that she took a step back. "*Help* you? After what you did to me?"

"What *I* did?" What was he talking about? *He* was the one who'd rejected *her*. He'd told her grandfather he couldn't marry her because of the rumors about her parents, the suspicions that they had been spies. He'd feared the unproven accusations could jeopardize his security clearance and taint his budding Naval career.

Which was ironic given *his* father's disreputable past.

She blocked off the familiar jab of hurt. She didn't care about the past. She didn't even care about the heartbreak he'd caused. None of that mattered. She had to save her grandfather—and to do that, she needed Coop's help.

"I'll pay double," she said. "Whatever you want."

"Forget it."

"But—"

"I said forget it." He turned on his heel and stalked off.

"But that car…those men." Her desperation swelled. She had to convince him. "Coop, please. They're chasing me. They're going to kill me. *I need your help.*"

The roar of the approaching car stopped her, and she spun back to the road. The sedan was just hundreds of yards away now, flinging up dust, rocketing toward the airstrip at breakneck speed.

She'd just run out of time.

Panicked, she whirled back to Coop, shifting from foot to foot. He'd paused halfway to the trailer and stood with his hands braced low on his hips, scowling at the oncoming car—but she couldn't take time to explain. He probably wouldn't believe her if she tried. No one else had—not the police, not the FBI, not her boss at the Madera Mountain nuclear lab where both she and her grandfather worked. Instead, they'd begun investigating *her*.

Unable to wait another second, she rushed past the flight shack to the nearest Cessna and peered through the open door. The key was in the ignition.

Should she try to fly it? She wasn't a pilot, but Coop had given her lessons that summer they'd spent together, and she'd watched him fly dozens of times.

Her gaze sliced back to the sedan zooming toward them, throwing up blankets of dust. And a terrible sense of certainty settled inside her. She had no choice. If she didn't leave now, she would die.

She tossed her knapsack into the cockpit, climbed up, and slammed the door. If she could just get off the ground without crashing, make it far enough away to escape those men...

"Hey," Coop yelled, loping back toward her. "What are you doing?"

Saving her life, she hoped.

Running on adrenaline, she reached down to check the fuel switch, racking her memory for what to do. She flipped on the master switch, pumped the primer with trembling hands, pushed in the red fuel mixture knob.

Then she turned the key to engage the propeller, and the old plane rumbled to life. Hardly breathing, she sent a nervous glance through the windshield, then cringed.

Coop reached the plane, his eyes thunderous. The black sedan veered closer to the airstrip, and her heart jackhammered into her throat. Ignoring Coop, she shoved in the throttle, started the plane rolling down the dirt runway while she grabbed hold of the yoke.

A sudden burst of gunfire made her heart stall. She swiveled around and looked out the passenger-side window. The sedan's tinted window was down, a lethal-looking rifle aimed at the plane.

More gunfire tatted out. She ducked, her pulse maniacal, and heard the staccato barks of an answering gun.

Was that Coop? Was he armed? She hoped so; no matter how painful their history, she didn't want him to get hurt.

Crazed with fear, she forced herself upright. She frantically worked the pedals to steer, trying like mad to speed up. She had to get airborne. She'd never outrun that car on the ground.

But then the cockpit door jerked opened. She gasped, but it was Coop. He clung to the door behind the struts as they bumped down the runway, a pistol in his right hand.

"Move over," he shouted.

Relief flooded through her. He was going to help her. She let go of the yoke and scrambled into the passenger seat as he swung himself into the plane.

"Keep us covered." He closed the door and thrust his gun at her.

"But I don't—"

"The safety's off. Just point it out the window and shoot."

She took hold of the pistol, which was heavier than she expected. Cradling it as carefully as lit dynamite, she twisted around, pushed open the window, then gripped the gun with both hands. The sedan swerved across the runway behind them, its front tires flat, rubber flapping as it sped through the dirt on its rims.

But two gunmen now hung out the passenger windows, their faces covered with hoods, their weapons trained on the plane.

She angled the pistol out the window and pointed at the car. The plane vibrated, making her arms shake, and she knew it was futile to aim. The best she could hope for was to pin them down—and try not to hit the plane.

She gritted her teeth and squeezed the trigger, then jumped at the earsplitting bang. Her hands flew up from the recoil. A spent cartridge shot from the gun. She steadied the gun, inhaled the harsh, sulfuric smell of gunfire, and pulled the trigger again. The men dove back inside the car.

For now.

The plane accelerated. The Cessna's engine roared. "Strap in," Coop shouted.

Zoe set the gun between the seats and tugged on her harness, but then a rapid series of *tats* reached her ears. She glanced out her window, shocked to see holes appear in the wing.

"They hit us." Horrified, she swung around to face Coop. "They shot the plane."

He grunted, his gaze on the instrument panel.

"Can we can still fly?"

"We'll find out." He adjusted the knobs, increasing the plane's speed even more.

She gnawed her cheek, watched his forehead wrinkle in concentration as he calmly worked the controls. And she realized with a start that he was used to this. He flew under enemy fire, risking his life all the time.

He pulled back on the yoke, easing the Cessna's nose up, and the plane lifted away from the ground.

She held her breath. Every muscle in her body tensed. The plane chugged, strained, slowly gained altitude. She gripped her seat, her fingernails gouging the cushion, her gaze glued on the desert sand.

Had the bullets hit something vital? Would the plane crash or explode in the air?

But long seconds passed and the plane stayed airborne. The desert floor slowly retreated. The propeller continued to spin.

She peeked out the side window. The sedan had stopped at the end of the runway. Three men stood beside it, black hoods covering their heads, their deadly weapons growing smaller as the plane soared into the sky.

Shuddering, she closed the window, then turned back to face Coop. They'd made it. They were safe—at least for now.

Assuming the plane stayed in the air.

"What do you think?" she asked. "Is the plane all right?"

"I don't know." He glanced at the damaged wing, then at the instrument panel again.

Her mind still reeling, her body shaking from the surge of adrenaline, she watched him work the controls.

Thank goodness he'd helped her. She never would have escaped those men alone. And she still couldn't believe he was here. But there he sat like a vision from her painful past, like some bizarre sort of déjà vu.

Her gaze drifted over the rugged lines of his face, the hollows of his dusky cheeks. His biceps bulged under the sleeves of his T-shirt. His shoulders rippled with strength. She eyed the powerful line of his neck, his flat, sexy stomach, the intriguing worn spots on his faded jeans.

A wayward thrill ran through her. He was still the most arresting man she'd ever seen. And he slouched in his seat in a posture so familiar it made her throat ache—his jean-clad legs sprawled wide, his booted feet working the pedals, his tough, sinewed hands managing the yoke with expert skill.

He turned his head, as if sensing her watching, trapping her with his gunmetal eyes. And his sexual appeal slammed through her, jumbling her stomach even more.

She'd never met another man like him. No one had ever affected her so intensely. No one had even come close.

"You all right?" His deep voice rumbled through her nerves.

Hardly. Her life had been turned upside down. Their plane could crash at any time.

And now she was flying through the desert with Coop, the man who'd demolished her heart.

But she managed to nod. "I'm alive at least."

Coop's gaze didn't waver. Instead, he narrowed one flinty eye at her, as if sighting down the barrel of his gun—reminding her that even though he'd helped her, he wasn't exactly her friend.

He would demand an explanation—and rightfully so. But how much should she say? Would he believe her if she told him the truth? None of the authorities had.

But what choice did she have? She had to convince him to help her. She only had thirty-six hours to pay that ransom. A delay could cost her grandfather his life.

She snuck another glance at Coop. The sharp intelligence in his eyes scrambled her pulse.

She'd managed to escape the assassins.

But she had the feeling her problems had just begun.

Chapter 2

Eight summers ago, Zoe Wilkinson had sauntered into Coop's life like the answer to his erotic dreams—and blasted his world apart.

Damned if she hadn't just done it again.

Cooper Kennedy tore his gaze from the brilliant blue sky beyond the Cessna's windshield and scowled at the woman who had loitered in his memory for years. She perched beside him, looking so innocent with her small, freckled nose and generous mouth, that stubborn, fine-boned chin. He raked his gaze down her slender throat, back to the sexy mole winking above her lip, and his hold on his temper slipped.

Innocent, hell. This woman had crushed his heart, screwed him over without remorse, done her best to destroy his dreams. And now she'd charged back into his life—still beautiful, still provoking those knight-to-the-rescue urges, still demolishing his hard-won plans.

He jerked his gaze back to the dashboard, appalled by what he'd just done. His orders had been clear. Stay at the airstrip. Watch for Leonard Shaw, the target of his surveillance. Phone his Navy contact the minute the AWOL scientist appeared.

He wasn't supposed to battle gunmen. He wasn't supposed to disobey orders. *Again*. And he wasn't supposed to be flying through the desert with Zoe, the woman who'd gutted his heart.

And who was the granddaughter of his target, to boot.

He gave her a look of pure disgust. She looked the same, all right. Still guileless, still dressed in those too-prim clothes, although the rush to evade those killers had taken its toll. He eyed her dusty, knee-length shorts, the wrinkled blouse buttoned tight to her chin. Her normally rigid braid had unraveled, and loose strands curled around her face.

The contrast used to intrigue him—the demure exterior that hid the erotic woman beneath.

Nothing about her amused him now.

The airplane's engine sputtered, drawing his attention back to the controls. He studied the instrument panel, then the holes in the starboard wing. *Just what he needed.* The right tank was leaking fuel and the fuel gauge didn't work—along with who-knew-what other parts. He had no business getting this death-trap airborne, especially with a passenger on board. If it weren't for their pursuers, he'd land this wreck right now.

He switched to the other wing tank and tossed Zoe a headset, waiting until she'd plugged it in. "Hand me the log book. It's on the floor."

She handed over the book, and he studied the entries, calculating the fuel in the undamaged tank. With luck, they could make it to Deadman's Junction, the nearest, good-sized town—assuming nothing else went wrong.

And what were the chances of that?

He checked their course with a hiss of disgust, then clamped his gaze on Zoe. "So what was that about?"

She turned her head to face him. This close he could see the fatigue bruising her skin, the anxiety lurking in her wide blue eyes. He didn't blame her for being afraid; that attack had rattled him, too. But those dark circles under her eyes hinted at something deeper, something that had kept her from sleeping for days.

Something that wasn't his problem.

"You probably won't believe me." Her throaty voice slid through him, kicking off a kaleidoscope of carnal memories, igniting his temper even more. That voice had always hit him like a sucker punch, so at odds with her schoolmarm looks.

His gaze dropped to the full curves beneath her tightly buttoned top. Curves he knew intimately. Curves he'd touched and stroked and licked...

His lips thinned. "Try me."

Nodding, she pressed her hand to her throat. *No ring.* No surprise. Few men could measure up to her intellectual standards. Certainly not Coop—the son of an alcoholic and a thrill-seeking hell-raiser from a dead-end desert town.

"It's...about my grandfather," she admitted.

Leonard Shaw. That figured. Of course he'd be involved in this mess.

And if anyone knew his target's whereabouts, it would be Zoe. "So where is America's premier physicist? Still busy collecting awards?"

"You've followed his work?"

"Nuclear science is a little over my head, princess. Wasn't that the point?"

Her face reddened, and she crossed her arms. *Good.* She deserved to feel guilty after the way she'd treated him.

He tightened his jaw, tamped down another flash of anger. Zoe was ancient history. She'd meant nothing to him for years. She was just a woman he'd known, one who'd entertained him the summer before he'd shipped out for boot camp. They'd flown in Pedro's planes, had some spectacular sex…

And if he'd acted like a besotted fool and bought her a ring…it hardly mattered now.

"The truth is," she began again, that husky voice doing unwanted things to his insides. "He's missing."

Coop tried to look surprised. "Since when?"

"Three weeks ago."

He knew that was true. The Navy had pulled Coop from his carrier squadron and banished him to the airstrip then. And while he hadn't wanted this assignment, he figured it was poetic justice. He could finally bring down the man who'd tried to ruin *him*.

He returned his attention to the instruments, but his thoughts lingered on Shaw. He had no trouble picturing the scientist as a traitor. Shaw was a user, a cold, domineering man determined to get his way—no matter whose life he destroyed.

But what about Zoe? Was she involved in the espionage, too?

Everything inside him protested the thought. The Zoe he'd known had been a crusader, intent on fighting injustice and righting the wrongs of the world—including the allegations that her parents had been spies.

Turned out he hadn't known her as well as he'd thought.

"At first I thought he'd gone geocaching," she continued. "He still does that every few weeks. He says hiking around the ghost town helps him clear his mind."

"I remember." Shaw's hobby had always struck him as odd—a grown man trekking around the desert, using his GPS to search for hidden caches filled with trinkets. But since that hobby had brought Zoe back to the desert with Shaw…

They'd fist met when they were ten. She'd come rock hunting with her grandfather. Coop had been doing odd jobs at Pedro's airstrip, desperate to ride in a plane. But then she'd fallen into a mine shaft at the ghost town, breaking her elbow, and hadn't returned to the desert for years—until the summer they'd both turned twenty-one.

"But he usually only goes for a few days," Zoe continued, drawing Coop's attention again. "When he didn't come back, I started to worry. And then Peter Ruegg called me in. He's head of security at our lab."

Captain Ruegg. Coop's contact on the surveillance case.

"My grandfather and I work together," she added. "At the Madera Mountain Naval lab. It's just outside of Ely."

Coop nodded. The Nevada lab had replaced Los Alamos and Sandia as the premier facility for nuclear research.

"Ruegg started asking questions—about where my grandfather had gone, how long since I'd seen him, whether I'd been in contact with him."

Coop checked the Hobbs meter to gauge the fuel. Satisfied, he slid her a glance. "Go on."

"The FBI has been on-site at the lab for awhile, investigating a data leak. And they…" She looked down at her hands. "They think my grandfather is involved. I think they suspect me, too." Her eyes swung back to his. "But he isn't a traitor, Coop."

Right. "Then why do they suspect him?"

Her eyes turned bleak. The steady drone of the engine filled the silence as he waited for her response. "Because he copied some of his work to a flash drive and removed it from the lab."

"That's a problem?"

"It's a felony. We're not even supposed to save our work to an external drive, let alone take it home."

The distress in her voice tugged at something inside him, kicking off a reflexive swell of compassion, but he ruthlessly shoved it aside. Zoe Wilkinson wasn't his problem. Her life, her worries had nothing to do with him now.

And no way would he give in to the urge to offer comfort, to press that soft, curving body next to his—no matter how defenseless she seemed.

Besides, he knew darned well she would lie to protect Shaw. She'd do anything the man asked. Hell, she'd dumped *him* fast enough.

Still fighting the sympathy she evoked, he scanned the approaching mountains and adjusted the altitude of the plane. Even if he wanted to believe her, her story had holes—such as, who had attacked them at the airstrip.

"So Shaw ran off with the flash drive," he prodded.

"Not exactly. He was kidnapped."

"Kidnapped?" Whatever he'd expected her to say, it wasn't that. "What makes you think that?"

"I got a note last night, a text message on my cell phone, demanding the missing data as ransom."

Coop snorted at that absurd tale. "And you think it's at the ghost town?"

"It has to be. I searched his apartment, his lab…it's the

only place left. He goes there all the time. He even keeps supplies out there. That's where I think he hid it—with his supplies."

He studied her pallid face, his mind reeling with doubts. Either she was a great actress, or she was telling the truth. But Leonard Shaw kidnapped? The Navy would have briefed him if that was the case.

And yet he had seen her assailants….

"Did you call the police?"

"No. It's…complicated." She let out another long sigh. "He's been acting strange lately, paranoid. He told me people were following him and trying to steal his research."

Coop lifted his eyebrows, but she shrugged. "He's always been secretive. A lot of scientists are. Competition in the field is fierce. And his project is classified, so he has to safeguard his work. But this was different. He acted scared, really frightened. And he kept warning me not to trust anyone—not the police, not our colleagues at the Navy lab, not even the FBI.

"And then, right after he went missing, Captain Ruegg called me in. The FBI questioned me, too. And men started following me, watching me… I don't know who they were. I assumed they were FBI." Her voice faltered. "They broke into my house. And I think they bugged my phone."

Coop's mind flashed to those black-hooded gunmen, and his belly turned to ice. "And you didn't report it?"

"Of course I did. I went straight to the police. They took the report, but they didn't seem to believe me. They acted suspicious, as if *I'd* done something wrong."

Coop shifted his gaze to the mountains rolling beneath them, their barren slopes pocked with ravines. On the surface, Zoe's story made sense. The authorities would definitely suspect her, given the rumors that her parents were spies. And those dark circles under her eyes hinted at long-term stress.

But he had a weakness where Zoe was concerned. She had a way of burrowing past his guard, making him want to protect her, even while she played him for a fool.

"So who were those men at the airstrip?"

"The kidnappers, I guess. I thought at first it was the FBI or someone from the lab. I know they had me followed. But when I saw those hoods..."

"But why would the kidnappers want to hurt you? Don't they need you to find the ransom?"

"I don't know." She flopped back in her seat. "None of this makes sense."

Coop felt just as confused. The whole story sounded bizarre, but he couldn't deny one thing. Those gunmen had tried to kill Zoe.

And if they weren't the kidnappers, who were they?

He frowned at the instrument panel, the misgivings he'd had about this surveillance case rushing back full blast. Everything about this assignment had been odd from the start. He'd only received the sketchiest of briefings. No one had bothered to send him updates. They'd just dumped him off at the airstrip, leaving him to spend three sweltering weeks watching the sun bake cracks into the ground.

And even stranger, why send a fighter pilot to do surveillance instead of someone from the FBI's anti-terrorist unit or Navy Special Ops?

He shrugged off the doubts. None of that mattered. He wasn't supposed to ask questions, wasn't supposed to think. Ignoring orders had landed him in this mess to begin with.

Or so he'd believed.

He'd been assigned this case as punishment after he'd disobeyed orders during a routine reconnaissance run. Of course, he'd had no choice. He'd had to enter that forbidden Syrian airspace to bail out a rookie aviator who'd gotten in over his head.

But the politically sensitive incident had coincided with a State Department visit to the Mideast region, embarrassing the Navy's top brass. They'd wanted the incident buried, the Syrians placated—and Coop promptly banished from sight. So when Naval Intelligence had needed a pilot to conduct surveillance at the isolated Nevada airstrip, Coop had been the unwilling choice.

He hadn't dared protest. He knew the penalty could have been worse. The Navy could have launched a Board of Inquiry, court-martialed him and booted him out. But someone up the chain of command had interceded and finagled the surveillance stint instead.

At least that's what he had believed.

Unless he'd been chosen for some other reason…

He quashed that disturbing thought. The reason he was here didn't matter. And his course of action was clear. He had to call this in, land the plane in Deadman's Junction and let the authorities deal with Zoe.

Or the Navy would ground him for good.

He reached for the switch on the radio. Zoe shot him a startled glance. "What are you doing?"

"Reporting the attack."

"But…you can't. I don't want the police involved."

He cocked his head, lifted one brow. "You want those men to get away?"

"No, of course not. But the police will detain me, question me. I told you they think I'm involved. And I don't have time. I've got to find that flash drive before the deadline runs out."

He hesitated, the urge to help her riding him hard. But

he had orders to follow—unequivocal ones. And for once in his life he couldn't ignore the rules.

He turned on the radio. Nothing. He flipped the switch, checking several other frequencies, but only got dead air. "This is nine five zero delta romeo," he called. "Requesting a radio check, any radio."

No one answered. He slumped back in his seat in disgust.

"What's wrong?"

"The radio's out." And he'd left his satellite phone with his survival vest back at Pedro's airstrip.

"You mean because of the gunshots?"

"No. The plane's just old, and Pedro didn't do much upkeep. The radio needs to be replaced." As did most of the other parts.

He eyed the monstrous peaks dominating the landscape below him, the surrounding foothills littered with rocks. Unease slivered through him, but he blocked it off. They would make it to Deadman's Junction. He had enough problems to contend with without conjuring up new disasters.

And speaking of disasters… His gaze traveled back to Zoe. She sat staring out the windshield with her shoulders hunched, her mouth set in a worried line. A section of hair had slipped from her braid and dangled behind her ear—making her look younger, softer, more vulnerable.

And suddenly, time stalled and he was twenty-one again, grinning at the sexy woman in those uptight clothes, the woman who'd turned him inside out. He'd been so crazy about Zoe, so determined to prove that he deserved her, that he could be what she believed he was—smart, decent, worthwhile.

She'd been way out of his league, a princess from another world. She'd grown up in a brilliant, famous family—with parents who didn't beat her, in a house where meals appeared like clockwork on the table, where life didn't revolve around the quantity of booze her old man had consumed.

And yet, she'd treated him as her equal. She'd respected him, admired him. Little wonder that he'd fallen for her hard.

But in the end, she'd done more than just reject him. She'd tried to destroy him, to deny him the one thing that mattered most. She'd had her grandfather use his connections to get Coop's appointment to the Naval Academy revoked.

The betrayal had shocked him, enraged him. But he hadn't surrendered his dream. He'd become a pilot the hard way—he'd enlisted, put himself through college, worked his tail off to make the top of his flight school class. And he'd finally succeeded. He'd earned his wings of gold, become one of the elite.

But he would never forget how she'd tried to harm him—no matter how innocent she currently seemed.

Suddenly, she scooted forward and peered through the windshield. "Coop, wait. We need to land."

"Why?"

"We've gone past Crater Canyon."

He lifted one shoulder in a shrug. "I'm not heading there."

"What?" Her gaze flew to his. "But you have to. I need to find that flash drive."

"After those men tried to kill you?" Was she nuts?

"I don't have a choice. I don't have much time to pay the ransom. And I can't let my grandfather die."

He stared at her, incredulity making his voice rise. "And what if they catch up? What then?"

Her face turned even paler, highlighting the freckles on

her nose. "They don't know where I've gone. The desert's huge. They'll never find me out here."

"The hell they won't. If they kidnapped your grandfather, they've studied his habits. They know he goes to Crater Canyon. You said he still flies there every month."

"I have to risk it."

"For God's sake, Zoe—"

"Don't you understand? They're going to kill him. And I can't trust anyone else. I tried. I went to the police. I talked to the FBI, but they all think I'm a spy."

Coop steeled himself against a surge of guilt. He was working against her, too. But he had to turn her in and let the authorities decide what to do. Her innocence—or Shaw's—had nothing to do with him.

"Forget it. I'm landing at Deadman's Junction. You can do what you want after that."

Her eyes filled with hurt. She plopped back in her seat and looked away. He scowled at her wounded profile, wanting to console her, believe her, but he refused to change his mind.

He couldn't. He'd die if he couldn't fly.

Just then the airplane lurched.

Zoe sat up straight. "What was that?"

"I don't know." He checked his watch, glanced at the undamaged wing. They shouldn't have run out of fuel.

The engine sputtered again, then died.

"What's happening?" Zoe asked, her voice rising. "Why is it doing that?"

Coop didn't answer. His pulse suddenly pounding, he shoved the throttle forward and cranked the starter. The engine rumbled briefly, then went dead quiet again.

The propeller slowed. Wind whistled through the cockpit. The plane made an ominous creak. They began to lose lift and the nose pitched down.

"Oh, God," Zoe whispered.

He spared her a glance. She sat bolt upright, staring out the windshield, her knuckles white on the seat.

"Tighten your seat belt and help me look for a place to land." He pulled back on the yoke, adjusting the pitch of the airplane to maximize the glide. Then he scanned the rocks beneath them, searching for a place to put down.

The plane steadily descended. His adrenaline ratcheted higher. All he could see beneath him were rocks. He scoured the boulders for an opening, his palms growing slick on the yoke.

"Over there," Zoe said. "I see a space."

"Where?" He glanced out the starboard side where she was pointing, spotted a narrow stretch of sagebrush between two high ridges of rocks. The strip was short, not much bigger than the landing deck on an aircraft carrier—minus the arresting wire to help them stop.

But he didn't have a choice.

He angled toward the opening, maintaining the best speed to glide. Then he jiggled the switch on the radio, hoping for a miracle, in a last-ditch effort to summon help. "Mayday, mayday, mayday. This is nine five zero delta romeo. We're a hundred miles south of Deadman's Junction, heading north with our engine out. Mayday, mayday, mayday."

Still nothing. *Damn.*

He tossed down the useless receiver, focusing fully on the landing now, his blood pumping hard in his veins. The plane glided lower. The sandy stretch came closer—but they were still too high to put down.

"I'm putting the plane into a slip," he warned Zoe. "We're going to fall fast, but don't panic. We'll be okay."

He turned the yoke and depressed the rudder, keeping the nose down to avoid a stall. The plane instantly plummeted, making his head light, like an elevator plunging straight down.

The ground rushed up. He eased off the controls.

They were committed now.

He glanced at Zoe, and the terror in her eyes filled him with regrets. "Brace for impact."

He pulled back on the yoke. The desert blurred past. He raised the nose and held. He gritted his teeth, working the rudders as the plane grew sluggish and slowed.

The rear wheels touched down. He strained to hold up the nosewheel, his back muscles rigid from the effort, sweat running into his eyes. But the nose slammed into the sand, digging in deeply, jerking them to a halt. "Hold on!" he shouted.

The plane's momentum yanked them into a cartwheel. They flipped end over end, the plane crumpling, the din of smashing metal deafening his ears. He hit his harness hard.

And his mood dove even more. He'd known from the start that Zoe would bring trouble.

And it had just gotten worse.

Chapter 3

Coop hung upside down in the shattered cockpit, his blood whomping through his skull, the stench of shorn-off metal stinging his nose. He swiveled around in his harness, spotted Zoe dangling limply from her seat beside him, and a fierce jolt of dread constricted his throat.

"Zoe! Are you all right?"

She moaned in response, and he closed his eyes in relief. She was alive, thank God. But she could be hurt. He had to get her out of the wreckage and check her for injuries fast.

Bracing his arm against the roof, he unlatched his seat belt and dropped awkwardly onto his back. He squirmed through the mangled metal, the hot afternoon air drifting through the gaping holes. At least they'd survived the crash.

So far.

"Zoe." He twisted around to reach her. Blood matted her hair, and he tensed.

"Coop?" Her voice was faint.

"Hold on. I'll help you down." He rose and wedged his shoulder underneath her to reduce the pressure on the belt. "Grab the strap so you don't fall."

"I've got it."

He propped her up, careful in case she had other injuries, and undid the clasp. But she fell against him, knocking him off balance, flattening him to the roof.

"Oh, God. I'm so sorry. I didn't mean to let go." She struggled to rise, shoving against his stomach, and he let out a grunt. "Are you all right?" she asked.

"Yeah." He inhaled to get his wind back, then managed to push to his knees. "How about you?"

"I'm fine."

He doubted that. A nasty scrape marred her cheek. Her scalp was bleeding, her wide mouth pinched with pain. His concern about her injuries grew.

"Come on. Let's get out of here."

"Will it explode?"

"Probably not. I doubt there's enough fuel left." He crawled through the opening where his door had been, then reached back and pulled her out.

Still holding her hand, he blinked in the blinding sunlight at the metal strewn over the sand. The fuselage smoldered behind them. The tail lay in a patch of sagebrush yards away. One of the wings had broken off and stood upright against the rocks like a macabre flag.

He wiped his sweaty face on his sleeve. The plane was toast. They'd have to hike out of the desert on foot—unless the Emergency Locator Transmitter worked and someone rescued them.

And given Pedro's aversion to maintenance, he had little hope of that.

He scanned the high, rocky ridges boxing them in, glad the landing hadn't been worse. If he'd overshot the opening or touched down a few feet to either side...

Shaking off that unnerving thought, he towed Zoe from the smoking debris. The brutal, midday sun broiled his scalp. Sweat moistened his spine, pasting his T-shirt to his back. Zoe stumbled behind him, and he stopped, then turned around to check her out.

Blood caked her hair above her ear. Her now-soiled blouse hung askew, with half of the buttons ripped off. Even her shorts fluttered loose, one leg torn clear up her thigh.

He ran his hands over her shoulders, her back, checking for injuries. "Does anything hurt?"

She shook her head, then pressed her hand to her temple and winced. "Just my head."

"It's bleeding." Leaning closer, he parted her hair and examined the oozing cut. "We'll need a bandage. How's your vision?"

"Fine."

"No blurring? Double vision?"

"No."

She still could have a concussion. He gently prodded her scalp, searching for lumps, then slid his hands down her arms. Her skin was smooth, soft, chilled despite the heat. He took her wrist, and her pulse sprinted under his thumb.

But her pupils were even and small, her breath steady and fast, reducing the chances of a concussion or shock. And he had no further reason to touch her. He should let her go, step back, focus on finding help.

But his feet stayed rooted to the sand. He skimmed his

hands up her arms, drawing her closer, drowning in her deep, blue eyes.

"I thought we were going to die," she whispered. Her bottom lip quivered. A sudden sheen brightened her eyes. And he knew she was fighting to hold it together, that the crash had scared her more than she cared to admit.

And he couldn't help but respond. He tugged her into his arms and held her against him, absorbing the tremors wracking her body, her uneven breath fanning his neck. He stroked her hair, her back, offering what comfort he could.

She hooked her arms around his waist, resting her cheek against his chest, and the feel of her broke through his guard. Maybe it was the trauma of the plane crash. Maybe it was the realization that they could have died. But the bitterness he'd harbored against her subsided, replaced by a swarm of emotions—tenderness, sympathy, regret.

She snuggled closer against him, her body still shaking from the adrenaline release. He closed his eyes and inhaled, absorbing her familiar scent. And he was suddenly, vibrantly aware of the feminine curve of her hips, the seductive fullness of her breasts, the taut thighs pressed against his. His reaction was predictable, uncontrollable.

Wrong.

He shifted away before she could notice. Sex with Zoe had never been the problem. She'd brought his fantasies to life and burned him alive. It was the rest that had come between them—their backgrounds, her grandfather, her lies.

Determined not to go down that road, he tried to lighten the mood. "I guess the landing was a little hard."

"A little?" She managed a shaky laugh. He brushed a stray tear from her scraped cheek, her brave, lopsided smile warming his heart.

And for an instant, time peeled away again, bringing back that flash of connection, that sense of rightness he'd always felt around Zoe.

But he shook it off and turned his attention to the sizzling sand. "There's some shade by that ridge. Think you can walk that far?"

She stepped further back and looked away, her moment of weakness gone. "I've just got a headache. How about you?"

"My shoulder's stiff, but that's about it." He rotated his right arm to test it. "It's just a bruise."

"So what do you think happened?"

"We must have run out of fuel." He squinted at the mutilated metal littering the sand. "Go wait in the shade. I'm going to hunt for supplies."

"I'll help."

"You need to rest. You could have a concussion."

"I said I'm all right. I'll rest later, after we've searched the plane." She turned on her heel, headed back to the wreck.

He frowned as she walked away, the torn shorts flapping against her thigh, and blew out a frustrated breath. She definitely hadn't changed. She was still determined, stubborn...

But she'd need that willful streak to survive. They could be stranded out here for days.

Not wanting to think of that possibility, he followed her back to the plane. But like it or not, he had to face facts. No one knew they'd left the airstrip except their attackers. His Navy contact, Captain Ruegg, might continue to ignore him for days. And even when someone finally missed them—or the plane—and mounted a search, the chances they'd be spotted were slim. Planes crashed in the wilderness all the time—and remained undiscovered for years.

While Zoe searched the sand around the airplane, he pried open the baggage door and retrieved the emergency kit. He quickly rummaged through it, unearthing a signal mirror and map, and some basic first aid supplies. There was also a moth-eaten blanket, four petrified granola bars, a baseball cap bearing an agricultural company's logo—and at the bottom, several vital quarts of water.

He exhaled, thinking longingly of his Navy flight vest with his survival gear. But he'd been working undercover at the airstrip, pretending to be on leave, so he'd stowed the vest in the shed. He'd figured his sidearm was protection enough.

Big mistake.

He stuck the ball cap on his head and crawled back into the plane. Bypassing the broken radio, he squeezed through the twisted metal, trying to see if the Emergency Locator Transmitter survived. But the cabin had pancaked on impact, and he couldn't wriggle through.

Giving up, he scooted back into the cockpit and hunted through the debris, then spotted his sidearm wedged under the dashboard with Zoe's cell phone. Feeling more at ease armed, he shoved his gun into his waistband and tried the phone.

No signal—hardly surprising on the desert floor. But if he climbed that ridge…

He exited the plane, spotted Zoe bending over her knapsack, and headed her way. But then he paused, struck by a sudden doubt. What if she refused to call for help? She'd had a fit when he'd tried the radio in the plane.

Unwilling to risk it, he slipped her cell phone into the pocket of his jeans. He'd give it back *after* he made the call.

Ignoring his protesting conscience, he retrieved the emergency kit, then started toward her again. She turned as he approached.

"I found my knapsack," she said. "I've got sandwiches and water."

"Good. I found some water, too." He angled his chin toward the rocks. "Let's take inventory in the shade."

"All right." She swung her knapsack over her back, and he plodded beside her through the sand, refusing to feel any guilt about concealing her phone. He had to call for help. They couldn't fool around out here. Desert survival wasn't a game.

"Watch out for snakes," he cautioned as they neared the ridge.

"I know." She lowered herself to the sand, sending a gecko scurrying into the sagebrush, and he dropped the emergency kit at her feet.

"I'm going to climb up the ridge and get our bearings. You can sort through what we've got."

She murmured her agreement, and he started climbing, still keeping an eye peeled for snakes. The sun blazed down on his head. Sweat streaked down his temples and stung his eyes. He scrambled over the sun-baked rocks, his breath coming fast, the hot, dry air desiccating his throat.

Minutes later, he reached the top. He blotted his face on the edge of his T-shirt, pulled out the cell phone, and turned it on.

No service. He frowned, switched the channel to roaming, but still couldn't pick anything up.

They were on their own.

His mood plunging, he stuffed the phone back into his pocket and braced his hands on his hips. To the east stood the mountain range they'd flown over—where Crater

Canyon lay. They'd landed in the rocky foothills to the west. Beyond the rocks lay the desert, the flat, gray sand stretching to the horizon a hundred miles away.

He sucked in the fiery air and scanned the endless, unbroken terrain. As he'd expected, there was no road, no sign of civilization in sight, just rocks and sagebrush. He sighed.

Not eager to break the bad news to Zoe, he climbed slowly down the rocks, then returned to where she sat in the sand. She'd divided the sandwiches, granola bars and water into two orderly groups. A third pile contained the first aid kit and miscellaneous supplies.

She raised her eyes at his approach. "What did you see?"

"Nothing."

"No road?"

"No." He lowered himself to one knee beside her, pulled the map from the pile, and spread it out. He found the area of Pedro's airstrip and slid his finger across the page. "We're about here, in the southern part of the Antelope Valley."

She scooted closer, her bare arm bumping his, and pointed to a dotted line. "Isn't that a road?"

"Yeah. But that's probably fifty miles away—and it's unpaved. I doubt it gets much traffic this time of year."

She nibbled her lower lip. Her worried eyes met his. "You think someone will search for us?"

"I doubt it. The radio didn't work. The Emergency Locator Transmitter might have sent out a signal if Pedro kept the battery charged...but his maintenance wasn't the best."

"So no one knows we went down."

"It's worse than that," he admitted. "No one knows we even took off."

"I see." Her voice sounded strained. She picked up the map with trembling hands. He could guess what she was thinking. There were plane wrecks all through these mountains—and the skeletons of people who'd never been found.

Closing the door on that grim thought, he grabbed the first aid kit and took out some antiseptic wipes. "Let's take care of those cuts."

She tore her gaze from the map and frowned. "They can wait."

"You don't want an infection, Zoe. We've got problems enough."

"I guess." Her forehead still furrowed, she set the map aside, leaned toward him and tilted her head. He parted the hair above her ear and cleaned the gash, then did the same to her cheek.

"Your cheek's just scraped. Ointment should be enough. But your head's still bleeding. We'd better wrap it with gauze." He took out the antibacterial ointment, put a dab on her cheek, then applied some to a length of gauze. More of her braid slid loose and slithered over his arm.

Trying to ignore the silky caress, he tied the gauze around her head. The frayed ends fluttered in the breeze. "There you go."

"Thanks." She shifted back, lifted a hand to the knotted gauze, and shot him a rueful smile. "I don't even want to know what I look like."

Kissable. The thought curved out of nowhere, sending a bolt of heat through his veins. He dropped his gaze to her lips, to that sexy mole at the edge of her mouth, and his blood made a ragged surge.

He shouldn't touch her. He knew that. She was injured, scared, and they had their survival at stake.

But sex with Zoe had been explosive. They'd shared a

summer he'd never forget. And damned if he didn't want to press his lips against hers and discover if she'd still make him burn.

He inched closer, his pulse heavy. She stayed riveted in place, her tongue moistening her lips. He angled his head, hunger rising inside him, desire crackling the desert air.

But then the hot wind gusted, whistling through the rocks behind them, stopping him dead. What was he doing? He couldn't touch Zoe. This situation was complicated enough.

He leaned back on his heels, appalled at what he'd nearly done. He had no business kissing Zoe—and not just because of the crash. The FBI wanted her for questioning. She'd once tried to ruin him. He couldn't forget his job.

Looking as awkward as he felt, she burst into a flurry of motion—folding the map, repacking the first aid kit, her eyes not quite meeting his. "You never said what you were doing at the airstrip," she said, loading the water into her knapsack.

Shrugging, he fed her the official line. "I took leave and came back to see Pedro. He wanted to visit his niece, so I told him I'd man the airstrip until he got back."

She nodded, as if accepting the story, and more guilt piled in his mind. The story should have been true. He should have come back to see Pedro. He'd visited him a few times through the years, but not nearly enough. Not as much as the old pilot deserved.

He shifted his gaze to the wrecked Cessna, the familiar call sign on the fuselage taking him back. He'd found Pedro's airstrip by luck. He'd been a dirty, nine-year-old kid, his scrawny frame covered with bruises, his stomach cramped with hunger, trying to run from his drunken old man. He'd hidden overnight in the flight shack, where Pedro discovered him the following day.

Coop's mouth kicked up at the memory. Pedro had fed him a breakfast of baked beans—the old pilot's meal of choice—then hired him to do odd jobs around the airstrip whenever he didn't have school.

And he'd changed Coop's life. He'd shown him that a man could be gentle, that not everyone who drank got violent and mean. And when he'd taken him up in that Cessna…Coop had discovered freedom, excitement. *Escape.*

"Then Pedro will miss you, right?" Zoe asked, drawing his thoughts back to their current plight. "He'll notice that the plane is gone and start a search."

Coop shook his head, reluctant to cause her more worry, but unwilling to give her false hope. "He won't be back for a couple of weeks yet."

"I see."

"Yeah." They were screwed. He leaned back against the rocks and let out a heavy sigh. "Is this all the food we've got?"

She grimaced. "Yes. It isn't much. The two sandwiches I brought and four granola bars that feel like concrete. They're ten years past their expiration date."

And they only had water for a day or two at most—which meant they should rest by day and hike at night to avoid the heat, especially since Zoe had banged her head.

But they couldn't risk staying by the plane in case their assailants caught up. He eyed the sizzling sand. "Do you have a hat?"

"In my bag."

"Put it on. We need to start hiking to that road. Or at least find a safer place to rest."

She pulled a straw hat from her knapsack, then fiddled with the brim. "Listen, Coop…I'm not going with you."

"What?"

She met his gaze. "I'm going to Crater Canyon."

The ghost town? He stared at her in disbelief. "Are you crazy?" Had the triple-digit heat scrambled her brain? "This isn't a game, Zoe. We could die out here. We have to get to that road and get help."

"I can't. I don't have time. I have to find that flash drive before the deadline runs out."

"The hell you do. Let the FBI handle this. They'll bring in a SWAT team and rescue Shaw."

"They'll never believe me. And if I hike to that road to get help, I'll miss the deadline." Her eyes pleaded with his. "Don't you understand? If I don't pay the ransom he's dead."

Coop's outrage rose. "So you're going to hike to Crater Canyon?"

"Yes."

"And what good will that do? Even if you find the flash drive, you'll still be stranded—and even farther from help."

"I know, but—"

"And what if those men come back? What if they're waiting up there?"

Fear flickered in her eyes, but she raised her chin. "I have to risk it. I'm not changing my mind about this."

He stared at her, too incredulous to speak. She really intended to go to the ghost town. She was out of her brilliant mind.

He rose and paced to a clump of sagebrush, his frustration increasing with every stride. She was insane, suicidal. Those men wouldn't give up; they'd lie in wait at the ghost town and gun her down for sure.

And what was he supposed to do? He couldn't make her change her mind or force her to hike to that road.

But neither could he forget his job.

Swearing, he kicked a tumbleweed out of his path. He didn't need this grief. Her problems were none of his business. And he definitely couldn't help her. The Navy and FBI wanted her for questioning. She was the target's granddaughter—and he had a job to do. He had to hike to that road, flag down a ride and let the Navy handle Zoe.

But what if she was right about the authorities? What if there was more to this case than he knew?

He yanked off his ball cap and plunged his hand through his hair. It didn't matter. If he screwed up again and disobeyed orders, the Navy would ground him for good.

He wiped the sweat from his face and glanced up, spotted two vapor trails streaking the brilliant Nevada sky—probably F/A-18 Hornets flying out of Fallon—and sudden panic squeezed his chest. He couldn't risk it. He couldn't jeopardize his career. He belonged up there— rocketing through the sky at mach speed, dogfighting and pulling Gs.

He shoved his cap back on and swung his gaze back to Zoe. She sat with her knees drawn up to her chest, her scraped cheek already puffy, her lopsided braid dangling around her flushed face. She looked defenseless, tired, determined.

His hopes dove. She wouldn't give up. He'd never convince her to go to that road.

And right or wrong, no matter what the consequences, he couldn't leave her out here alone.

He tipped back his head and closed his eyes, calling himself every kind of fool. Hadn't he learned from the past? This woman had screwed up his life.

And now, against his better judgment, he was about to let her do it again.

Chapter 4

The mountains kept moving.

Zoe squinted at the brown peaks shimmering in the haze, her head floating with fatigue, the fiery air a blowtorch on her throat. They'd been hiking toward those peaks for hours now, trudging over uneven rocks, roasting in the relentless sun—and the mountains kept dancing away.

She stumbled, barely managing to stay upright, and stole another glance at Coop. He strode silently beside her, his jaw locked in an angry jut, his lug-soled flight boots bludgeoning the rocks, broadcasting his hostility with every move.

He didn't want to be here. And she didn't need the aggravation of his bad mood. Her temples ached; her scraped cheek throbbed. Worry about her grandfather tormented her thoughts.

"There's shade up ahead," Coop said, his voice curt. "We'll stop there and drink some water."

Her spine stiffened at his bossy tone, his take-charge attitude ticking her off. But her protests died in her scorched throat. No matter how much she longed to argue, he was right. They needed to rest. She was dangerously dehydrated. And bickering over who was in charge wouldn't help.

He was also right about something else, although she refused to admit it to him. This journey defied common sense. They were hiking with too little water in lethal heat, heading to a ghost town even farther from help—where killers might be lying in wait.

Fear scraped her spine at that thought, but she pushed aside her concerns. She couldn't worry herself into a frenzy, couldn't conjure up disasters at every turn. She had to stay calm, deal with one dreadful problem at a time.

"This is good," Coop announced. He stopped in a sliver of shade and set the emergency kit on the ground.

She dropped her knapsack beside him and propped her hands on her knees. Sweat streamed down her face. A wave of dizziness made her head spin. Dark spots pirouetted in her vision.

She heaved in the blistering air, then made herself stand upright, unwilling to let him see her fatigue. If she showed any sign of weakness, he would insist on turning around.

He handed her a bottle of water, and she drank greedily, the warm liquid ambrosia on her raw throat. She gasped, caught her breath, and guzzled the water again. They hadn't even reached the mountains, had an entire night of hiking ahead of them, and she was already growing too weak.

Coop pulled the blanket from the emergency kit and folded it over the rocks. "We'll sit on this. The hot rocks will make us sweat too much."

Too exhausted to comment, she plopped down beside him on the scrap of fabric, her hip pressed against his. She handed him the bottle of water, trying to ignore his wide shoulder nudging hers, the brush of his corded arm.

He tipped back his head, and her eyes followed the movement, tracing the muscular line of his throat. Her gaze lingered on the black scruff coating his jaw, the jet-black hair peeking from beneath his cap. She pressed her palms to her thighs, the sudden urge to touch him throwing her off guard.

"How far do you think it is to the mountains?" she asked to distract herself.

"Another hour, maybe. It'll take us most of the night to hike to the ghost town. Those hills are steeper than they look." His electric eyes met hers, making her heart sprint. "We'll have to rest at some point, too."

Afraid he'd see her unruly reaction, she peered at the mountains again. Angry or not, he was a seriously sexy man. But she couldn't compound her mistakes, couldn't start fantasizing that he wanted to kiss her—like that moment when he'd bandaged her head.

She brushed some dirt off her shorts and tried to corral her scattered pulse. But the subtle touch of his shoulder, the feel of his hard thigh pressed against hers made it difficult to breathe.

"Here." He held out the bottle of water.

"No, thanks. I'm good."

"You'd better drink up. People have died out here with water in their canteens."

"All right." She took the bottle and sipped the warm liquid again.

"So when is that ransom due?" he asked.

"Midnight tomorrow." A familiar spurt of panic skittered inside her. She only had thirty-one hours to get to the ghost town and find the flash drive, then deliver it to the rendezvous point halfway across the state.

"And you really think that flash drive's at the ghost town?"

"It has to be. I've looked everywhere else." She inhaled sharply, refusing to consider what would happen if she was wrong. "My grandfather has kept supplies out there for years—his sleeping bag and tent, even an ATV. He goes there so often—at least once a month—and he didn't want to lug stuff back and forth. I'm sure that's where he hid the flash drive—with his supplies."

Coop took the water bottle from her and closed the cap. "So let's say you find it. What then?"

"I go to the rendezvous point."

"Where's that?"

She hesitated. She trusted Coop, but she couldn't take any risks with her grandfather's life at stake. Too much could still go wrong. "The kidnappers will let me know."

Coop lifted his brows, his skepticism clear. But she couldn't tell him everything—at least not yet. She took off her wide-brimmed sun hat and fanned her face.

"So exactly what's on that flash drive?" he asked, his voice neutral.

"I'm not sure."

"You must have an idea."

"Yes, but I can't really discuss it. The information is classified, and I signed an oath."

His mouth tightened. "I have a top-secret clearance."

Of course he would. She couldn't stop the swift shaft of hurt. "I know how important that is to you."

His eyes hardened. "What does that mean?"

As if he didn't know. She pressed her knees to her chest and hugged her legs. Coop had ended their affair because of that clearance—or rather the rumors that her parents had been spies. He'd feared any link to her family could harm his budding Naval career—and the top-secret security clearance he'd eventually need.

But her parents hadn't been traitors. The accusations had been lies. And she'd thought that with his family's background, Coop would have understood.

That hardly mattered now, though. Ignoring the old hurt, she turned her mind back to the missing flash drive. "I don't work on his project, but he has been trying to do the same thing all his life—find a way to recycle spent nuclear fuel rods. He's trying to leach out the waste, then concentrate and reuse the uranium."

"I thought they could already do that."

"They can. They've developed a few different processes, but they all require expensive equipment, centrifuges, special reactors—and it still leaves dangerous waste." She stuck her hat back on her head and angled the brim against the sun. "He's trying to invent a simpler procedure, one that's cheaper, more portable."

Coop leaned back on his hands and stretched out his muscled legs. A tear slashed the knee of his jeans. "And why is that important?"

"It would be better for the environment, for one thing, a way to reuse the nuclear waste that we've got piling up. Storage is always a problem. Security, too. You've seen the trains." They passed through the desert on their way to the Navy's repository in Idaho under heavy military guard.

Coop's forehead creased. Insects buzzed in the shimmering heat. "So who would want this technology?"

"It depends on the process, the level of refinement. But the government would definitely want it. The military, too. That's why they're funding his research."

"Could it be used for weapons?"

A frisson of dread shivered through her, turning her throat dustier yet. "Possibly. I won't know until I examine the information on the flash drive." But Coop had voiced her biggest fear—that her grandfather had invented something dangerous, something catastrophic. Why else would someone kidnap him?

"You think he succeeded?" Coop pressed.

"I don't know. I'm sure he's made progress. But a breakthrough..." She shook her head.

"Then why was he so secretive?"

"The project's classified, for one thing. And a certain amount of paranoia comes with the job. There's never enough funding for research, so competition is fierce. No one wants a colleague to steal their idea." She lifted her hand and let it drop. "And he's worked on this procedure his entire life. He's determined to prove his doubters wrong. It would kill him to give it up."

The project drove him, obsessed him. Everything had always come second to his research—even Zoe, the orphaned granddaughter dumped on his doorstep when she was fourteen.

But she understood that naked ambition, that burning desire to succeed. Her parents had been slaves to their research before they'd died, too.

Even Coop had cared more about his job than her. He'd dropped her for fear her reputation would taint his career.

She glanced at his noble profile, his high cheekbones bronzed by that golden skin. And she had to admit that wasn't fair. Coop hadn't been ambitious. He hadn't cared about fame or rank. He'd just loved to fly. He'd lived it, breathed it, had a genius for it. Pedro had told her Coop had the most natural talent he'd ever seen.

A born risk-taker, Coop had lived for the thrill, the freedom, the speed. Flying had been his ticket out of the desert, a way to escape the loneliness of his life.

The same loneliness that had lurked inside her.

Unwilling to continue down that old track, she staggered to her feet. "We'd better get going."

He frowned up at her. "You can't push the pace in this heat. It catches up to you fast."

She agreed. She longed to lie down and sleep, but she couldn't afford to waste time. "I'm not that tired."

He rolled to his knees and stuffed the blanket and water back into her knapsack. Despite her intentions, she couldn't help but admire the powerful flex of his biceps, his wide shoulders shifting under his T-shirt, the sinews standing out in his arms.

And a sudden thought occurred to her. "How come you don't wear your Naval Academy ring?"

His head came up. His gaze turned so hostile that she blinked. "Is that a joke?"

A joke? "No, of course not." The Navy personnel she worked with always wore their rings—not while doing research, but certainly when they left the lab.

He surged to his feet and stalked off without answering, the emergency kit tucked under his arm. She grabbed her knapsack and trailed him, trying to keep pace with his rapid strides.

Why was he suddenly angry? What had she said to set him off? He'd sounded just as furious at the airstrip when he'd hurled that accusation at her. But she'd never done anything to harm him.

"Coop, wait," she called, hurrying to catch up. "What's wrong?"

He wheeled around, his gaze slamming into hers. "You know damned well I didn't go to the Academy."

"What?"

He turned on his heel and strode off. She stood motionless, gaping at his retreating back, too stunned by his words to move. He didn't go to the Academy? But that didn't make sense. It was all he'd ever talked about. He'd told her he'd spent years after high school trying to get accepted—studying, hiring tutors, retaking the SAT multiple times in an attempt to boost his score. And when he'd finally made it…

He wouldn't do anything to jeopardize his appointment—even marry her.

Still reeling with disbelief, she rushed after him, her lungs sawing in the heat.

"But why not?" she asked when she reached his side.

"Don't play dumb."

"But I don't—"

"You want to talk about this? Fine." He stopped, his eyes burning black with anger, fury pouring off him in waves. "Did you think I wouldn't find out what you did—that you got my appointment revoked?"

"Revoked? Me?" Her jaw turned slack. Incredulity made her voice rise. "I did not."

"Your grandfather then."

"But that's…that's crazy."

"Crazy?" he scoffed. "He warned me to stay away from you, told me you wanted to be left alone. But I never thought you'd go that far."

She gaped at him, confusion mingling with shock. "You're wrong. How can you say that? That's not what happened at all."

"The hell I am." He leaned toward her, his eyes blazing, the planes of his face rock hard. "I'm not wrong about the letter I got rescinding the offer."

"But my grandfather wouldn't have—"

"Pedro contacted some people he knew at the Academy. No one would admit it publicly, but a certain physicist had connections on the admissions board. And they suddenly decided I wasn't Academy material after all."

Her mind couldn't grasp it. "But that's… I can't believe it."

"Believe it, princess. It's the truth."

Her stomach churned like an advancing tornado. Everything inside her protested his words. But she couldn't deny the certainty in his eyes. He'd lost his appointment to the Academy.

But if what he said was true…

"I never said that," she whispered, shaken. "I never wanted you to leave me alone." Dear God. She'd adored Coop, loved him. "My grandfather said he'd gone to talk to you, to find out what your intentions were. And he told me…you said…"

She choked down her pride, forced the words out. "That I was just a fling, someone to…spend time with until you could leave for the Academy." Only he'd put it far more crudely, to her shock. "And that with my parents' past and the security clearance you'd need, you'd never marry me."

Deep lines bracketed his mouth. His voice turned harder yet. "And you believed that?"

"No. I didn't. Not at first. I was devastated. I came to see you at the bar that night. You remember… You were with someone else."

He held her gaze for several seconds, then folded his

arms. "Shaw said you thought I was beneath you, that you wanted me to leave you alone."

"Never." A horrible sense of betrayal seeped through her. She didn't want to believe that her grandfather had meddled in their relationship—and lied to them both. But Coop believed it. She could see the conviction in his eyes.

And no wonder he despised her. To lose his appointment, everything he'd worked for...

"But it doesn't make sense. Why would he do that? He knew how much I cared about you."

Coop snorted. "I wasn't good enough for you, obviously."

She shook her head, still not able to accept it. Her grandfather loved her. He wouldn't have intentionally hurt her—especially after the devastation of her parents' deaths.

And Coop's rejection had crushed her. It had taken her years to fully recover, years before she'd even dated again. She'd finished her PhD early, dedicated herself to her research, feeling dead inside, numb.

But if what Coop said was true, then he had suffered, too.

She swallowed with effort, placed her hand on his iron bicep, felt the tension rippling his arm. "Coop, I'm sorry. I still think there's a mistake, that something else happened, but just so you know...I never would have hurt you."

He stared at the ground, working his jaw, and the sick feeling swirling inside her increased. "Forget it. It doesn't matter now."

Of course it did. This misunderstanding had ruined their relationship, irrevocably changed both their lives.

And anger still rang in his voice.

But she nodded and dropped her hand, knowing there

wasn't much else she could say—at least until she had more facts.

They resumed hiking toward the mountains, the silence between them only slightly less hostile, her thoughts in turmoil from what he'd said. And she kept sifting through the memories, trying to make sense of what went wrong.

She'd come to the desert that summer because of her grandfather's health. He'd just had a pacemaker installed, and she hadn't wanted him too far away. But after a few trips to the ghost town had assured her of his strength, she'd stayed in their rented trailer, spending her days studying while he wandered off on his hikes.

Until she'd seen Coop again—and realized that the scraggly boy she'd met at the airstrip when she was ten had turned into a gorgeous, virile man. Her studies instantly forgotten, she'd spent long, wonderful days hanging around the airstrip, riding through the desert with him on his Harley—and even more blissful nights in his arms.

Her grandfather hadn't cared for Coop. Coop had lacked everything the elderly scientist valued—education, culture, academic prestige. He hadn't seen Coop's drive, his potential, or the tender way he'd treated her. Still, her grandfather hadn't seemed too concerned—until she'd told him they were nearly engaged.

But would her grandfather have lied to her and betrayed her trust to break them up?

She gave wide berth to a clump of cactus, the brutal sun frying her head. No matter what Coop believed, she couldn't see it. Her grandfather was a hard man, self-absorbed, driven by his ambitions—but he loved her. He wouldn't have caused her such pain.

Would he?

A hot, edgy feeling stirred inside her. She didn't want to

believe it. She could never forgive a deception that terrible, one that had caused her such wrenching pain.

But regardless of what her grandfather had done—or not done—in the past, he had a lot to answer for now. Why had he hidden that flash drive? What had he feared so much that he'd jeopardized both their careers? And why had he put her in this predicament—with killers on her heels, the FBI suspecting her of treason, the kidnappers' deadline fast running out?

Fighting her growing anger, she kept plodding over the rocks. The mountains still taunted her from a distance. The sweltering sun shimmered off the desert floor, creating mirages on every side. The parched air sucked her sinuses dry, gluing her tongue to the roof of her mouth.

Without warning, Coop stopped. She staggered against him, and he threw out his arm to break her fall. "What's wrong?" she asked, panting.

"A helicopter. Someone's coming."

To rescue them—or something worse? She glanced up, squinted into the blazing sky, raising her hand to shield her eyes. "Where? I don't see—"

"Come on. Let's get behind those rocks."

He grabbed her arm to help her. Her fatigue abruptly forgotten, she dashed with him to a pile of rocks. He nudged her between two boulders, and she squeezed through the narrow space.

"Who is it?" she asked, breathless.

"I don't know yet."

He set down the emergency kit and crouched beside her. She tilted her head, straining to hear, and finally picked up a helicopter's rhythmic whomp.

"Don't move." He inched up, peered over the top.

"What do you see?"

He didn't answer. The deep reverberations grew louder.

Unable to bear the tension, she rose and peeked over the rock, ignoring his warning frown.

She scanned the sky and spotted a gray speck approaching in the distance. It neared their plane wreck, hovered over the crash site for several moments, then headed straight toward the rocks.

Coop jerked her down, and she huddled against him, her heart stuttering hard in her chest. Had the gunmen found them? Had the FBI or police caught up?

"Don't signal," she pleaded. "Please, Coop. I need time to find that flash drive."

His brow furrowed. The drum of the rotors grew louder. He opened the emergency kit and pulled out the mirror. Then he hesitated, the battle he waged clear in his eyes.

The helicopter thundered closer. She kept her gaze on Coop's, silently begging him not to move. A shadow passed overhead, the deep vibrations rattling her teeth.

Seconds ticked by. The noise faded away. And she sagged against the rock in relief. He hadn't signaled that chopper. He really was going to help her.

But all warmth disappeared from his eyes. He stood. "Let's go."

Hurrying to her feet, she followed him out from behind the rock. "You think they'll come back?"

"Count on it."

"But who was it? Could you tell?"

"The Navy."

"The Navy?" Had someone from the lab followed her to the airstrip? But she would have noticed another car. Unless… "Are they looking for you?"

"No."

"But—"

"I said, let's go." His eyes simmered with anger, impatience, and something else. Guilt?

She blinked, her thoughts thrown into disarray. Why would Coop feel guilty? What was he hiding from her?

He picked up the emergency kit and started hiking. She followed more slowly, suddenly besieged by doubts. Surely she could trust Coop—couldn't she?

She scrambled across the rocks behind him, her trepidation increasing with every step. Was there some other reason Coop had helped her? Another reason he'd jumped into that plane?

No, that was ridiculous. Coop was a fighter jet pilot. He had nothing to do with this case. He'd come back to visit Pedro, and then she'd dragged him into this mess.

And she was getting as paranoid as her grandfather, imagining danger where it didn't exist.

But eight years had passed since she'd seen Coop. In all that time he must have changed.

She grimaced. He hadn't changed that much. And if he was hiding something, he was probably doing it to protect her, to keep her from worrying too much.

But as she trudged behind him in the sweltering heat, eyeing the pistol tucked into his waistband, her apprehension remained. She'd trusted her grandfather—and Coop had thrown that trust in doubt.

What if she was making the same mistake with *him?*

Chapter 5

He'd officially lost his mind.

Coop stood on an outcropping of rocks halfway up the mountain, certain he'd gone insane. There was no other explanation for his behavior. He should have flagged down that chopper and seized the chance to be rescued. Where had he stuffed his brains?

"Any sign of that helicopter?" Zoe called from behind him, sounding anxious.

"No." He looked out at the purple sky streaking the horizon, the silhouettes of mountains hundreds of miles away. Never mind that Zoe had begged him not to do it. He should have ignored her plea, signaled for help, and ended this crazy ordeal.

Appalled at his lapse in judgment, he turned to face the woman who'd turned his mind to mush. She perched on a rock in the encroaching darkness, devouring one of the sandwiches she'd packed. The white gauze around her head gleamed in the twilight. Her braid drooped off center, the loose strands dangling around her face. Her scraped cheek had mottled over the past few hours, adding to her wretched look.

And despite his lingering resentment, his conscience berated him even more. She should be in a hospital getting fluids and X-rays—not making a long, dangerous hike up a mountain in the dark.

Still shaking his head at his attack of insanity, he strode back through the rocks and scrub brush to the boulder where she sat. He flexed his aching shoulder, stretched his throbbing back.

"What's wrong?" she asked.

Everything. "My shoulder's just stiff." He perched next to her on the rock, took the sandwich she held out. "Thanks."

"I hope it's okay. It's hummus and alfalfa sprouts."

He shrugged. Not his usual fare, but he was hungry enough to eat sand.

He dug into the sandwich, devouring a third of it in one gulp, and his mind swiveled back to his case. He could justify running off with Zoe at the airstrip. With those would-be assassins trying to kill her, he'd hardly had a choice. But then he'd headed for the mountains instead of the road and hidden from his rescuers—which definitely looked bad. Still, the Navy would forgive everything if he found that computer flash drive.

And turned in Zoe.

His mood plummeting at that thought, he polished off the rest of his sandwich, then reached for the water she'd propped between them on the rock.

"Do you want this?" She held up one of the petrified granola bars from the emergency kit.

He unscrewed the cap on the bottle. "We'd better save it. We might be out here for awhile."

"Right." She dropped the granola bar into the knapsack at her feet and sat back up. "Was that really a Navy helicopter?"

"It had the right markings." It also made sense. The Navy ran Madera Mountain, the lab where Zoe worked. So even though the FBI was leading the investigation, the Navy provided support—planes, equipment, manpower such as Coop.

"But how did they know where I went—and that our plane went down? You said the Emergency Transmitter might not have worked."

He took another swig of the warm, stale water and gulped it down. "They could have followed you to the airstrip."

She shook her head, and the white gauze bobbed in the dusk. "I don't think so. I would have noticed the dust trail if there'd been another car."

True enough. He shifted his gaze to the vast, empty desert darkening below them. Nothing moved in that fishbowl unseen.

Including them.

Was someone watching them and monitoring their progress? Apprehension trickled through him at the thought.

"I saw some jets fly by earlier," he said. "They might have spotted the plane and called it in. Or someone could have come to the airstrip and found your car."

"But how did they know which way we were heading? And why didn't they come back when they saw the plane wreck to see if we were all right?"

All good questions—with no simple answers. He pinched the bridge of his nose, the mounting uncertainties too strong to ignore. Why didn't that helicopter land and check for survivors? Why hadn't they mounted a full-blown search? And if the Navy *had* spotted their tracks—and knew they were alive—why didn't they return? Unless they'd left them out here to die....

He scoffed at that bizarre thought. He couldn't let his imagination run rampant, conjuring motives that didn't exist. The Navy had sent a reconnaissance aircraft. It was his fault they hadn't been found.

Now he had to hightail it to that ghost town, hope he could catch a signal on Zoe's cell phone, and turn her in.

If their assailants didn't kill them first.

Shutting down that dire thought, he slid a glance at Zoe. "How's your head?"

"Not bad."

He knew that wasn't true. She'd looked exhausted before the plane crash, and they hadn't stopped hiking since. But she hadn't complained, had done her best to keep up. And he couldn't help but admire her resolve.

He scowled at the shadows creeping over the desert. The cool breeze brushed his skin. He didn't want to like Zoe. He didn't want to respect her spirit, her determination. And he didn't want to sympathize with her—or believe her version of the past.

But he was having a hard time holding on to his anger. He turned his head. Their gazes clashed in the dusky night, and his pulse took off at a sprint. Those baby-blue eyes sucked him in, demolishing his willpower, impossible to resist.

And that complicated everything.

He took another long pull of water. The trilling of a screech owl carried on the air. Regardless of the past, he had to figure out what to do with her now. Maybe he could convince her to hand over that flash drive. It would redeem him with the Navy if she did.

He tapped the empty plastic bottle on his thigh, determined to try. "Look, Zoe, if that helicopter does come back, you need to turn yourself in."

"I can't do that."

"Why not?"

"Because they'll never believe me."

"I'll vouch for you. I'll make sure they rescue Shaw. And if you give them the missing data, they'll know you're on their side."

She shook her head. "You don't understand."

She had that right. "What's there to understand? You're out of your depth here. You saw those men. You can't fight them alone."

"I know it seems crazy."

"It *is* crazy."

She sighed and crossed her arms. "Let me put it this way. What's the most important thing in your life?"

He didn't have to think about that one. "Flying."

"Would you ever give it up?"

"No." It was what he did, who he was.

"Well, that's how my grandfather feels about his work. This project is his life. It's what he lives for, what drives him. It always has.

"And for him to do something this drastic, to put everything he cares about at risk… Either he's gone totally nuts or there's a reason, a good one. And I can't trust anyone until I know for sure. Not the FBI, not the Navy, not the police. There's just too much at stake."

"I get that. But what if he *is* nuts? Or what if he's involved in something illegal? You're still willing to risk your life?"

"I have to. At least until I know what's on that flash

drive." She exhaled again, more heavily this time. "Look, Coop. I know he isn't always nice, but he's my family, the only one left. I can't turn my back on him."

"I'm not asking you to abandon him. I'm saying you should let the professionals handle this."

"I know." Her gaze held his. "And I'm not expecting you to help me. I understand if you can't get involved. But…just give me a chance to get away, all right? Don't tell anyone you saw me, at least for a couple of days. Not until I can figure this out."

He didn't want to help her. He still didn't fully trust her. And he had a job to do. But neither could he put her in danger—and let her face those gunmen alone.

No matter what he did, he was screwed.

Feeling trapped, he turned his face to the sky. Venus winked near the horizon. A few stars gleamed overhead. There'd be millions soon, a glittering universe beckoning him, luring him to adventure, escape…

Zoe placed her hand on his forearm, and the soft, warm feel of her branded his skin. "I meant what I said, Coop. You really don't have to help me. And I…I still think there's a mistake, but if my grandfather had anything to do with you losing your appointment to the Academy, I'm sorry."

His gaze met hers in the gathering darkness. His heart tapped an off-kilter beat. He skimmed her full, feminine lips, that tempting mole, the alluring curve of her throat.

And guilt returned with a vengeance. If she'd told him the truth about the past, then Shaw had lied to them both, manipulating Zoe for his own ends. And if he'd done *that,* then he could also be using her now.

Which meant she had nothing to do with the espionage case—and Coop had no right to withhold the truth. She deserved to know about his surveillance job, the real reason he was here. She'd been forced into this mess the same as he had.

That was a big *if,* though. And until he had proof, he couldn't assume that she wasn't involved. The truth could send her running, ruining his chance to locate the flash drive or Shaw—and save his career.

But although he couldn't come clean yet, he could accept the olive branch she'd held out. "I understand why he didn't want us to marry. I wasn't much of a prize back then."

"How can you say that? You were great." The indignation in her voice made his mouth curve up. So she was still a crusader, still fighting for the underdog.

"Hardly. You saw where I lived." A dilapidated trailer in a dirt-poor town. "He probably thought I'd end up like my old man."

"He didn't know you like I did."

That was true. Coop had let down his guard with Zoe, allowed her into his heart—something he hadn't done with anyone since. "I was broke. I had four years at the Academy ahead, then flight school, assuming I made it that far."

"Still—"

"I'm not defending him." Far from it. Shaw had tried to ruin his life. "I'm just saying I understand his thinking."

"He had no right to deceive us, though. *If* that's what he did."

"He did." And now Coop was deceiving her, too. More guilt roiled inside.

She pulled her hand away. The lonely yips of a coyote rose from the desert floor, echoing his pensive mood. He cleared his throat, gazed at the emerging clusters of stars. "Just so you know, though. That night…when I was at the bar—"

"You don't have to explain."

"Yeah, I do." He shifted around to face her, met her soft eyes darkened by night. "I was furious. I got drunk. I picked her up, took her home, and left her there. Nothing happened."

Drunk or not, he could still remember every moment of that night—staggering out of the bar, blinded by fury, Shaw's words flaying his mind. That he was worthless. That Zoe thought he'd never measure up. That she hadn't had the heart to tell him, but she wanted him to leave her alone.

Shaw had known exactly where to strike him, discovered his most vulnerable spot. And when Zoe had appeared at the bar that night, Coop's pride had made him lash back.

But maybe he shouldn't have believed Shaw so quickly. Maybe he should have spoken to Zoe at the bar. Maybe he should have pressed harder to learn the truth instead of believing a man he'd despised.

He exhaled, regrets settling inside him like an anchor hooking in deep. It didn't really matter now. All that was in the past. It was better to forget it, move on, concentrate on their current mess.

"So did you ever get married?" she asked, her voice husky.

"No." There had been women over the years. Not as many as she probably thought. None serious. "I move around a lot with the Navy, so I'm not in one place long." Truth be told, Zoe had set a standard no one could match. He'd never felt that connection with anyone else.

"You?" he asked.

She made a wry smile. "I'm married to my work, I guess."

Her work. Right. The reason they were here.

She shivered in the chilly air and rubbed her bare arms. "You'd better put on your sweatshirt," he said. "It cools off fast out here."

"What about you?"

"I'll live."

She rose, took the sweatshirt from her bag and shook it out, then pulled it over her head. But it snagged on the knotted gauze.

"Hold on. You don't want to knock that bandage loose." He walked over, stretched the neck of the sweatshirt, and helped slip it over her head. Her soft hair slid over his fingers, like satin brushing his skin.

"Thanks." She reached up to pull her braid free, just as he grabbed the bottom of her sweatshirt and pulled it down. His knuckles grazed her breasts, and he froze.

Their eyes locked. Coop's blood made a heavy surge. And he was excruciatingly aware of how close she stood, that her warm, lush lips were just inches away from his.

He needed to move, step away. He couldn't succumb to the urge to kiss Zoe. But everything inside him clamored to touch her, feel her, taste her again…

He loosened his grip on her sweatshirt, his gaze not wavering from hers. Unable to resist, he reached up and curled his hand around the nape of her neck, stroking her throat with his thumb. She was so soft, so sensitive, so inviting.

She quivered beneath his touch. Her gaze dipped to his mouth, kicking off a frenzied stampede in his chest. The air backed up in his lungs.

He should let her go. *Go. Go. Go.* The thought bleated in his mind, like a jet's collision system warning of imminent impact. This was the wrong place, the wrong time. Zoe was off-limits, part of his surveillance case. *Taboo.*

But he never had obeyed the rules.

He tugged her even closer, his mind turning fuzzier yet. For years Zoe had been his fantasy—lush, sultry, hot. She had a face like an angel, a body made for sin.

And memories began to bombard him, chipping away at his resolve. The musk of her naked skin. The sensual jolt of her kiss. The husky little moans she'd made in the back of her throat.

"Coop," she whispered. Her provocative voice held him captive. His gaze arrowed straight to her mouth. Her full lips parted, her tongue darting past that alluring mole, beckoning him, tempting him.

One little kiss couldn't hurt.

He lowered his head, fused his mouth with hers. She tasted sweet, erotic, just as he remembered. He sank into the kiss, every male synapse firing to life, and the helpless sound she made aroused him even more.

He angled his head to deepen the kiss, and the feel of her torched any doubts. He widened his stance, ran his hands down her back, cupped the perfect flare of her hips.

She shuddered and trembled against him. Her arms tightened around his neck, bringing her breasts closer against his chest. And beyond the hunger, beyond the primal urges pulsing inside him, something long-forgotten awoke. A feeling of rightness. A deep sense of satisfaction he hadn't experienced in eight long years.

Then a horned owl cried, its low hoots piercing the night. Coop dragged up his head, his breathing labored, struggling to come down from the kiss. What was he doing? He couldn't get involved with Zoe. He still couldn't fully trust her. He couldn't compound this mess.

He forced himself to step away, shocked at the effort it took. The dazed look in her eyes didn't help.

He plowed his hand through his hair, cleared the

thickness from his throat, shaken by the intensity of that kiss. "We'd better go." Before he lost all control and took her where she stood.

"Right." The huskiness of her voice nearly did him in.

"And put your hat back on. If anyone's looking for us, that white gauze will give us away."

Forcing his feet to move, he strode back to the boulder, the need for her battering his blood. He tucked the emergency kit under his arm, swung Zoe's knapsack over his back, and set off into the dusk.

He'd wondered if she'd feel the same. Now he had his answer.

And he wished he hadn't found out.

As far as mistakes went, that kiss had been a doozy.

Zoe staggered after Coop up the mountain hours later, her head still whirling, so overwhelmed with lust that she could hardly hold on to a thought.

Lord, but that man could kiss. She'd tried to put her reaction into perspective, to chalk it up to a moment of mutual insanity, but she couldn't get the rough, thrilling feel of him out of her head—the erotic scrape of his jaw, the iron muscles bunching under her palms, his arousal pressing the apex of her thighs. Thick. Hard. Huge.

She closed her eyes on a sigh, aching to touch him again. She tripped and stumbled forward.

Coop wheeled around and grabbed her arm. "Careful." His deep voice rasped in the darkness, sparking another flurry of nerves.

"Thanks." Her voice came out breathy, to her chagrin. Her face flaming, she straightened, giving thanks for the cover of night. Bad enough that his kiss had reduced her to a muddled wreck. She didn't need him to know.

He turned away and continued hiking, the full moon painting him with silver light. She trudged up the rocky slope behind him, eyeing his broad, sturdy back, the relentless power in his strides—and struggled to gather her scattered sense.

So she was human. So she hadn't been kissed like that in years. Eight long years, to be precise. It was little wonder she longed to inhale his sexy scent, press her hot, naked skin to his deliciously muscled frame.

She quickly quelled that rogue thought. No doubt about it. That kiss had demolished her concentration, resurrecting needs she'd repressed for years. But it had been a mistake. A big one. She had no business thinking about sex when her grandfather's life was at stake.

But that kiss…

"We're almost to the top." Coop's deep voice floated back to her in the crisp air. "We'll rest there until dawn."

"I'd rather keep going." Not only did she need to find that flash drive, but she'd be less tempted to touch him that way. "The ghost town can't be too far away now. I checked the map when we stopped to eat."

"It's just over this peak. About a mile away." He stopped, pointed to something off to the side. "But see that?"

She paused to catch her breath and spotted the outline of a shack. "What about it?"

"It's part of the old gold mine. We're on top of it now."

"So?"

"So there are all kinds of hazards in the brush around here—caved-in mine shafts, machinery, rusty nails. It gets even worse closer to town."

"We've done all right so far."

"Yeah, but the moon's about to go down. We won't have any light when it does."

She didn't discount the dangers. She'd plunged through a mine shaft at the ghost town when she was ten and broken her arm. Her grandfather had stopped bringing her to the desert after that.

"But what about those gunmen?" she argued. "Shouldn't we sneak into town at night in case they're there?"

"If they're already at the ghost town, we're dead."

"What do you mean?"

He wiped his face on his sleeve. "The first thing they'll do is take the high ground and post a sniper to pick us off. And if they've got night vision devices, we don't stand a chance."

"But then—"

"I'm hoping we can beat them there. We know they aren't behind us. So they're approaching Crater Canyon from the other side. That means they'll park below the mountain where the road's washed out and hike in on foot. And that buys us some time."

"All the more reason to keep going."

"Not if we fall down a mine shaft. We can't go stumbling around the mountain in the dark. It's too dangerous. We have to wait until dawn."

She understood his reasoning. And she desperately longed to sleep. Her feet had gone numb. Her thigh muscles spasmed from fatigue. But her grandfather was in far worse danger than she was. She didn't have time to relax.

Coop continued hiking. She followed, scanning the rocks angled like abandoned tombstones on the moonlit hills. A few scruffy pine trees clung to the barren slopes, their twisted branches clawing the night.

It pained her to think that her grandfather was out there

somewhere—frightened, worried, alone. But not for long. No matter how tired she felt, she was going to rescue him.

But could she depend on Coop to help?

She hauled air to her scorching lungs and forced herself to consider the question she'd avoided all night. She wanted to rely on Coop. He was strong, smart, armed. He had the military training and survival skills she lacked.

But he didn't want to help her. He wanted her to turn herself in. And she had no right to involve him in her nightmare. He'd already fended off killers and crashed an airplane. She couldn't keep asking him to risk his life, especially for a man he didn't like.

Besides, no matter how wonderfully he'd kissed her, no matter how much she'd adored him in the past, she still had the sensation that she couldn't trust him, that he was holding something back. Sure, he'd evaded that Navy chopper at her request—but could she depend on him to do it again?

So what should she do? Leave him behind? She balked at the though—because he was right. Those men could be waiting at the ghost town. And no way did she want to take them on alone. She didn't even have a gun.

But neither could she ignore that flash of guilt she'd seen in Coop's eyes. Because if there was any chance he wasn't what he seemed…

She plodded up the mountain behind him, her mind flip-flopping through options, conflicted about what to do. She couldn't risk getting injured. Her grandfather needed her to survive.

But she also had to meet the kidnappers' deadline. She couldn't waste time sleeping, couldn't let those gunmen beat her up the hill. And she couldn't take the chance that

Coop had a hidden agenda and might be working against her somehow.

She steeled her nerves, made up her mind. She had to leave Coop and go it alone.

But how? She couldn't just stroll away.

Or could she?

Wheezing, she pushed the button on her watch to illuminate the dial. Two o'clock. Just a few more hours until dawn.

If she was going to make a break, she had to do it soon.

"I thought we were going to stop," she said.

Coop halted a few yards ahead of her and glanced around. "Yeah, this looks good. We can rest here for an hour or two."

"Great." She straggled to a stop beside him, her legs quivering so hard she could barely stand. They'd reached a small, flat section of ground near the summit. Boulders walled in one edge of the clearing, creating the perfect cover for her escape.

Coop set down her knapsack, pulled out the threadbare blanket from the emergency kit, and spread it over the ground.

"You'd better drink more water," he said.

She opened her mouth to argue, but then gave in. The sooner Coop fell asleep, the faster she could leave.

Trying not to groan, she lowered herself to the ground. She sipped from a bottle of water, then set it aside to leave with Coop. That done, she lay back to wait for her chance.

Coop stretched out beside her, his big body throwing out tempting warmth, and she bit back a sigh. She could do this. She could lie here with Coop and pretend to sleep.

She could ignore the nearness of his body, keep her mind focused on the task ahead—and off that amazing kiss.

And she could make it to that ghost town and find the flash drive before her pursuers did.

She wriggled her hips to move a small stone poking her back and stared up at the dazzling array of lights in the sky. "I'd forgotten how many stars you can see in the desert," she murmured, then yawned.

She'd forgotten a lot of things over the years. The tender way Coop had teased her. The acceptance she'd felt in his arms. The sheer fun she'd had—flying in Pedro's planes, clinging to Coop on his beat-up Harley as they raced down the desert roads.

And when he'd touched her...

She rolled her head to the side and studied his profile—his high-bridged, masculine nose, the slant of his sculpted cheekbones, the heavy growth of whiskers now covering his throat.

She'd never known another man like him. He hadn't cared about her disgraced family. He'd had no expectations of how she should act. He'd simply accepted her.

He was the only one who had.

Her gaze lingered on his corded forearms, then traveled back to his sensual mouth. That kiss had brought it all back—the excitement, the freedom, the heady idea that she could push the limits, forget her family's reputation, and live her life for herself.

But he'd been right to break off that kiss. They led different lives now. She wasn't even sure she could trust him. And she definitely didn't need her hormones distracting her with her grandfather's life on the line.

But as she listened to Coop's breathing deepen in the darkness, more doubts piled inside. If it was right to go on without him, why did it feel so wrong?

Chapter 6

Zoe's scream jolted Coop from sleep.

He rolled to his feet in a rush of adrenaline, his gun out, his senses instantly alert. Where was she? What happened? He whipped around and scanned the shadows, tension coiled deep in his gut.

Silence pulsed in the predawn darkness. The cold morning air grazed his face. Barely breathing, every muscle primed to fight, he skimmed the boulders at the edge of the clearing, the sagebrush swaying in the breeze.

There was no sound, no movement. No sign of Zoe. But he hadn't imagined that scream.

He crept toward the hulking boulders, his gaze trained on the night. Had she been injured? Captured? Why had she left the campsite?

He spun back and spotted the emergency kit by the blanket—but her knapsack was gone.

His stomach went into a free fall.

She'd wandered off on her own.

Disbelief spiraled through him, followed by an explosion of rage. Of all the reckless things to do! He'd warned her to wait until daybreak. Didn't she understand the dangers out there?

Judging by that scream, she'd just found out.

His gut turned to ice at that stark thought. He strode to the boulders, wanting to slam his fist into something, his fear for her out of control. But he couldn't charge after her blindly. He had to calm down and think this out.

She would have gone straight across the mountain to the ghost town, which was a mile away behind a ridge. But to reach that ridge she had to maneuver through a minefield of hazards—old cisterns, caved-in mine shafts, dangerous ravines…

Foreboding swarmed inside him, but he ruthlessly stomped it out. He couldn't let emotions cloud his thinking. He had to focus on rescuing her fast.

He hurried back, retrieved the remaining water from the emergency kit, then set out toward the ridge. A rabbit scuttled from his path into the sagebrush. A bird trilled and chattered nearby. He prowled silently down the hill, his gun in hand, scanning the obsidian landscape, past a hut on the verge of collapse.

Questions thrummed through him with every step. Why had she left? Why had she ignored the dangers? Why hadn't he realized she'd sneak away?

Guilt penetrated the anger, and he knew he was partly to blame. He'd underestimated her. He'd misread her level of desperation. He'd figured she'd eventually see reason, realize she couldn't rescue Shaw alone, and agree to let the authorities take charge.

But why would she? She thought the authorities were as dangerous as her assailants.

And what if she was right? What if someone in the government *was* trying to kill her?

Quickly rejecting that idea, he crept past some machinery skulking in the shadows and a mound of mine tailings grown over with shrubs. A coyote howled in the distance, sending a chill shimmying up his spine.

It wasn't that he trusted the authorities. Just the opposite. He'd had run-ins with the law growing up, butted heads with his superior officers in his career. But Zoe's suspicions didn't make sense. Her grandfather worked in a Navy lab. The government already owned his research. They had no need to steal his work.

He detoured around a prickly pear cactus and shook his head. Nothing about this case made sense. And if he had any brains, he'd get out now. Zoe had just handed him the perfect excuse. He could hike down the mountain, contact Captain Ruegg, and honestly report that she'd escaped while he was trying to bring her in.

In fact…he could call for help now. This high up he might catch a signal from a cell phone tower. He stopped, tugged Zoe's cell phone from his pocket, and turned it on.

A signal bar appeared.

His heart sped up. This was it, his chance to escape. He could call Captain Ruegg, bring in the cavalry to rescue Zoe, then hightail it back to his job.

Unless Zoe was right.

Unless the authorities *were* involved.

He hesitated, a flurry of doubts holding him in check. Because the fact was…Zoe was smart. She wasn't given to outlandish conspiracy theories. If she suspected that the government was behind this, he couldn't shrug those suspicions off.

No matter how absurd they seemed.

And he realized something else. Eight years ago, he'd made a mistake. He'd ignored Zoe's pleas to talk, refused to find out the truth behind her grandfather's claims. He'd been so proud, so ruled by the chip he'd carried on his shoulder that he'd refused to believe the woman he'd loved. Instead, he'd walked away.

He couldn't make the same mistake now.

Not with someone trying to kill her. Not with Shaw and that flash drive missing. Not until he could guarantee she'd be safe.

He blew out his breath and stuffed the cell phone back into his pocket, wondering if that plane crash had addled his brain. Or maybe it was that kiss. Because he sure seemed to have lost his common sense.

Shaking his head in derision, he started hiking again. Dark mounds appeared in the landscape. Dawn was beginning to break, turning the sky more purple than black.

And then a low moan reached his ears. He stopped, his heart hammering fast, and peered ahead. The cool mountain breeze brushed his face. Sagebrush rustled nearby. He waited, listening intently, the deep stillness torturing his nerves.

But then he heard it again. A groan—coming from somewhere on the left.

"Zoe?" he called softly. No answer. His pulse quickening, he tried again. "Zoe?"

"Coop?"

He closed his eyes. His breath came out in a rush. "Where are you?"

"Down here, in this canyon. I fell and I can't get out."

Her voice sounded muffled and strained. And the fear he'd held at bay crashed back full force. Because the thought of Zoe injured…

He unclenched his jaw and forced a calm into his voice that he didn't feel. "Hold on. I'm coming."

Heading toward her voice, he continued walking until he spotted the canyon's black slash. Then, careful not to get too close, he knelt and peered over the edge.

The canyon was narrow, deep, its bottom hidden in darkness. Sheer stone slabs lined the sides. Zoe stood below him on a wooden platform connected to a railroad trestle built to bring ore hoppers out of the mine.

She looked up, and even from a distance, he could see her fear. "I tried to climb up," she said. "I made it to this platform, but the rest of the way's too steep."

He studied the angle of the rocks beneath him, and his hopes sank. She was right. She'd never make it out this way. And he didn't have a rope to pull her up. They might find an alternate route when the sun rose, but they couldn't afford to wait. If their enemies were anywhere near this mountain, her scream had tipped them off.

"How does that trestle look?" he asked.

She turned around. "Not good. It's falling apart…but I can't see it very well."

Neither could he—but the little he could see looked bad. Still, that trestle was their only hope.

If it held their weight.

If it crossed the canyon to the other side.

If their pursuers didn't catch up and shoot them first.

He exhaled. Risky or not, they didn't have much choice.

"Stand back. I'm coming down." He stuffed his pistol into his waistband, shoved the water bottle into his back pocket, then scooted over the canyon's rim.

Moving carefully, clinging to weeds and rocks as he scrabbled for footholds, he lowered himself down the cliff. Loose soil rained onto his head. His arms and shoulders shook from the effort it took not to slip. He gritted his teeth, blinking the sweat from his eyes as the platform inched into view.

Close enough. He twisted around and leaped the final distance, landing with a heavy thud. The impact jolted his knees and made his teeth clack. He sprang back up and turned to Zoe.

She looked even more miserable close-up. Dirt covered her face. The gauze around her head was gone, her hair a scraggly mess. Her eyes were huge, betraying her fear, despite the determined angle of her jaw.

And it took every ounce of strength he had not to pull her into his arms and rage at her for endangering herself, for the terrible chance she took. But he bit back his angry words, muzzling his temper with effort. He'd have it out with Zoe when they were safe.

Still struggling to control his emotions, he studied the rotting bridge. The support beams looked intact—as far as he could tell—but most of the cross boards had disappeared. They'd have to walk on the beams without a handrail, keeping their balance the best they could—like crossing on a high wire over a black abyss.

He swung his gaze back to Zoe. "Think you can make it over the bridge?"

"You think it's safe?"

No, but what choice did they have? "It's worth a try."

"All right then."

"You're sure?"

"Yes." She lifted her chin, a glint of challenge stealing into her eyes—like the Zoe he used to know.

"The left side looks the strongest," he decided. He

grabbed on to the support beam and tested the board. "Follow me and step where I do."

He started across the beam, holding his arms out for balance, probing the boards for Zoe. The canyon began lightening below him. The sky turned a deep navy blue. He glanced back and watched Zoe hobble across the bridge behind him, her fear obvious in the rising light. "Are you all right?"

"As long as I don't look down." She managed a shaky smile, and another tendril of warmth snaked through his heart. The summer they'd spent together, he'd loved throwing her a dare—watching that chin come up, that glimmer of determination enter her eyes. She'd always been game for any escapade he'd wanted to try.

Especially in bed.

Heat jolted through him at that thought, but he clamped a lid on it fast. He wiped his brow on his sleeve, turned his mind back to the beam, checking for weak spots as he crept along.

The sky continued to brighten. The cool breeze gusted, carrying the scent of dried grass. He edged past the halfway point, and a large section of cross boards disappeared, creating a precarious, four-foot gap.

"Be careful here," he warned. "Wait for me, and I'll help you across."

He jumped over the unstable section, stretched back and grabbed Zoe's hand. She leaped across, then clung to his arm to get her balance back.

Suddenly, a man appeared below.

Coop froze. He squeezed Zoe's hand in warning while his gaze narrowed in on the man. The newcomer had black hair, black clothes and an AK-47 slung over his back.

One of their assailants.

He must have heard Zoe scream and entered the canyon

from the other side, closer to the road—just as Coop had guessed. But where were the other men?

Seconds ticked past. Coop stayed immobile, his hand locked on Zoe's, afraid any motion would tip their pursuer off. The man scoured the floor of the canyon, apparently searching for footprints, then started striding away.

Coop hissed through his teeth, let go of Zoe, and crossed the last few yards of the bridge. He stepped safely onto the dirt, turned back and reached for Zoe.

She hurried toward him, her hand extended toward his. But then the beam beneath her feet cracked. The sharp report shattered the silence. Coop lunged out and grabbed her hand.

The timber swung loose. Zoe stumbled, gasped. He jerked her off the trestle and fell with her to the bank, just as the man below them spun back.

Gunfire barked out. Coop whipped out his pistol, his pulse chaotic, and shoved himself to his knees. "Run!" he urged Zoe.

He took aim, fired at the man to pin him down, giving her a head start. Then he rose and raced after Zoe.

She sprinted up the ridge, limping badly, and ran down the other side. He hugged her heels, plowing through grass and bushes behind her, leaping over cactus and rocks. Their attackers knew where they were now. The sound of those shots would have carried, alerting anyone for miles around.

They skidded through the cemetery behind the ghost town, dodging tombstones and an old iron fence. Zoe angled across the field, heading toward the saloon, then stopped.

"There's a root cellar around here somewhere," she said, sounding breathless. "That's where he keeps his supplies. I remember that it's behind the saloon."

She whipped around, searching the area, while he watched for signs of pursuit. "There it is!" She hurried toward a bank of dirt.

Still keeping a wary eye on their surroundings, he followed her to the root cellar. She reached for the lock on the door.

"You know the combination?"

"His birthday. He always uses the same one."

The lock sprang apart. Zoe pulled open the wooden door and hurried down a flight of stone steps.

Coop tramped down the steps behind her into a dim, musty room with a packed dirt floor. Low wooden beams supported the ceiling. Bowed shelves lined the walls. A shovel leaned against a rubber storage container in the corner—Shaw's supplies.

Zoe wiped her face on the tail of her blouse and blew out a shaky breath. "That was close."

"Close?" Was she nuts? She'd tipped off their assailants and nearly gotten them killed.

And suddenly he couldn't hold it in anymore. He stalked over to her, the fear he'd suppressed rising inside. "What the hell were you thinking, running away like that?"

She stepped back and crossed her arms. "I was trying to help you."

Help him? "How? By falling off a cliff?"

"I didn't plan to fall. And you'd risked your life enough. I didn't think it was fair to keep asking you to help."

"Not fair?" His grip on his temper slipped. "For God's sakes, Zoe, I risk my life for a living. Flying jets is dangerous."

"But you choose to do that. You didn't ask to get involved in this."

No, he hadn't asked to get involved. And he didn't want to be here. He didn't want to risk his job, didn't want to care about Zoe again.

But damned if he could help it.

Which meant she was stuck with him, like it or not.

He leaned closer and grasped her chin, his anger about to explode. He wanted to intimidate her, shake some sense into her, force her to listen to him.

But the softness of her skin demolished the remnants of his control—bringing back the mind-blanking fear, the terror when he'd heard that scream.

"Damn it, Zoe." His voice came out rough. "Don't ever do that again. Do you hear me?"

And before he could reconsider, he jerked her hard against him and slanted his mouth over hers. The kiss wasn't gentle, wasn't nice—and he didn't want it to be. He plundered her mouth, ravaged her lips, giving vent to his fury, his frustration, his need.

He knew he should stop, let her go. They had to get out of here fast. But he drove his tongue in deeper, demolishing any restraint, laying waste to his lingering sense.

She'd nearly died. He'd nearly lost her—again. And the fierce sense of possessiveness rolling through him, the need to keep this woman safe made his rage burn higher yet.

He drew back, grappling with his rocketing emotions, knowing he was out of control. "I'm in this thing until *I* decide I'm out. You got that? And from now on you don't leave my sight."

Her face flushed, her eyes flashing fire. He knew she didn't like taking orders.

Too damned bad.

She jerked away and stalked across the cellar toward Shaw's supplies, and he knew she'd gotten the point.

And so had he.

He was in this gig for the duration.

No matter what the cost.

Chapter 7

Zoe hobbled across the musty root cellar, furious at Coop's high-handed manner, still reeling from that torrid kiss. Excitement rippled through her. Her pulse skittered like water in a broiling hot pan. The feel of his mouth devouring hers, the low, male growl he'd made deep in his throat had ignited a torrent of hunger, making her so turned on she could hardly walk.

She shivered, fighting to control the erotic sensations, to ignore the lingering feel of his lips. Thrilling or not, she couldn't let him boss her around. This was *her* problem, *her* grandfather who was missing. But it was hard to drudge up any resentment when she ached to fling herself into his arms.

She gave her head a hard shake, trying to forget the kiss, forget the desire sweeping through her, forget Coop's annoying tendency to take charge. None of that mattered—not with those would-be killers close by.

That grim thought scattered the lust, jerking her back down to earth. Determined to stay firmly grounded, she swept her gaze around the shadowy room. If her grandfather had done what she suspected, he'd placed the flash drive inside a container—a cache—and hidden it near his supplies.

She limped around the room on her tender ankle, scanning the hard dirt floor, the dusty, wooden shelves lining the walls, the low, timber beams overhead. But the cache was nowhere in sight.

Panic spurted inside her, but she made herself stay calm. The flash drive had to be here. She'd already searched everywhere else—his office, his apartment, the lab.

She double-checked the shelves, peered behind the storage tub—and then she saw it. A fake rock in the corner on the floor.

"I found the cache." She rushed over and picked it up, then pulled the plastic sides apart.

The flash drive wasn't there.

Her heart took a sickening nosedive. She stared at the cache—empty except for a folded sliver of paper—in utter disbelief.

It wasn't there. *After all she'd been through.* She'd been shot at and chased by gunmen, suffered a plane wreck she'd barely survived. And she only had eighteen hours left to pay that ransom. What on earth was she going to do?

"Do you have the flash drive?" Coop demanded from behind her.

Her heart plunging at the thought of Coop, she forced herself to meet his eyes. He stood where she'd left him by the steps, covered in dust, his expression forbidding.

He was about to get even more annoyed.

Shifting her weight from foot to foot, she looked down

at the empty cache—the cache they'd risked their lives to find. "No. It's not here."

Silence pulsed between them. Still clutching the cache, she closed her eyes, unable to believe she'd been wrong. She'd been so sure…

"Where is it?" he finally asked.

"I don't know." It never occurred to her that it wouldn't be here. "But he left a note."

She set the fake rock on the shelf and unfolded the paper. Coop joined her from across the room. He leaned over her shoulder, his nearness adding to her nerves. Her grandfather's note made her hopes sink even more.

He'd written down two sets of letters: *Se, C, Au* and *H, Cr, Cl.*

"What does that mean?" Coop asked.

"It's an offset cache."

"Meaning?"

She grimaced, reluctant to break the bad news. "He hid the flash drive in a different location. These letters are a clue to where it is…like a puzzle or a scavenger hunt."

He shot her an incredulous look. "He's playing a game when his life's at stake?"

She shrugged, unable to fault his outrage. Of all the times for her grandfather to create a puzzle, this was the worst.

"He knew he was in danger, that people were following him. He probably worried that this cache would be breached. And he knew I'd understand these letters. They're symbols from the periodic table of elements. It's a game we played when I was young."

Which meant he'd set this up, made it easy for her on purpose—because he wanted her to find that cache. But then why not confide in her from the start? Why not tell her about his troubles instead of making vague, paranoid comments that didn't make sense? And why put her in this terrible danger, leaving her to fend off her attackers alone?

"We can't take time to look," Coop said. "Those men know where we are now. We've got to get out of here before they block our escape."

He was right. Those gunmen would catch up at any time.

But how could she leave without the flash drive? If she didn't hand over the ransom, her grandfather would be killed.

"I just…I'll look through his things, just in case." He wouldn't have put the flash drive there—it was too obvious—but if he wanted her to find it, he'd have left a GPS. She stuck the paper in her pocket, knelt by the rubber tub, and made short work of the lock.

"He keeps an all-terrain vehicle in the shed by the saloon," she told Coop. "It's how he gets around out here. The key should be taped to the bottom of that gas can." She angled her chin toward a plastic can beside the tub.

Her grandfather had spent years exploring this area, first hunting for fossils and minerals, later geocaching when that hobby came into vogue. And each time he'd come, he'd added to his supplies. She opened the lid, and the sight of his familiar canvas backpack gave her another jolt. She closed her eyes and sent up a silent entreaty that he be safe.

Coop reached into his pocket, pulled out a bottle of water, and unscrewed the cap. While he drank, she searched through her grandfather's supplies—his sleeping bag and flashlights, books about minerals and rocks. As she'd expected, the flash drive wasn't there. But she did find the handheld GPS.

Because she'd lost her knapsack in the canyon, she stuck

the GPS into her grandfather's bag. Then she rose, took the water Coop offered and guzzled it down her dry throat. She gasped for breath, wiped her mouth on the back of her hand, and took another heavenly pull. The water was stale and hot, and she'd never tasted anything so good.

Coop stuffed her grandfather's bottles of water into the backpack along with the flashlights and tossed it over his back. "Grab the gas can, and let's go."

"All right." Her thirst marginally less desperate, she rose, threw the empty bottle into the tub, and grabbed the plastic can. Her ankle throbbed as she crossed the room behind him, but she ignored the pain. They couldn't afford to slow down.

Coop paused at the bottom of the stairs and raised his hand, palm out. "Stay here until I'm sure it's clear." He tugged out his gun and crept up the steps.

Zoe waited, her gaze on Coop's dusty flight boots, her thoughts swinging back to those men. Where were they? *Who* were they? And how were she and Coop going to get down the mountain without running into them?

"Come on up," Coop called softly.

She hurried up the stairs and into the open air. Feeling exposed now, vulnerable, she glanced around the hill behind the town.

The sun was steadily rising, turning the sky a brighter blue. She scanned the dried brush dotting the hillside, the ramshackle wooden buildings that comprised the abandoned town. She slid a wary glance in the direction of the canyon and suffered another attack of nerves.

Those gunmen could be anywhere—over the ridge, lurking in the wooden buildings, preparing an ambush on the road out of town…

"We're dead meat if they've got the high ground," Coop muttered, echoing her thoughts. "Come on."

He set off toward the shed, and she hurried behind him, crunching through the tall, dry weeds. Still favoring her tender ankle, she stepped over scattered boards and broken glass, trying not to make any sound.

Coop stopped behind the shed. She squeezed in beside him, her breath shallow and fast. He leaned closer, his warm arm brushing hers.

This close she could see the black lashes fringing his eyes, his irises shot with pewter sunbursts, the beard stubble roughening his bronzed skin. Even filthy, with his hair uncombed and dusted with dirt, he appealed to her too much.

"Wait here," he mouthed.

His gun raised, he crept through the weeds, keeping his back to the saloon. And she was intensely grateful he was here. Because if he hadn't rescued her from that canyon, if she'd had to do this alone...

Coop peeked through a broken window, then inched around the front of the building toward the dirt road winding through town. A few seconds later, he jogged back.

He set the backpack beside the shed. "Is the ATV in there?"

"It should be."

"Top off the gas tank and get it ready to go, but keep it inside the shed. You stay in there, too, where you won't be seen."

"Where are you going?"

"To sweep the area, see if I can locate those men. I don't want to drive into an ambush."

"But what about the flash drive?"

"We don't have time to look." He started for the saloon again, then shot her another hard stare. "I mean it, Zoe.

Stay inside the shed until I get back." He edged around the saloon and disappeared.

She worried her bottom lip with her teeth, glancing at the empty ridge behind her, then the gray, weathered buildings on either side. *First things first.* She unlocked the shed and pulled the backpack inside.

The shed was stuffy and small, her grandfather's old ATV taking up most of the space. Leaving the door partially open for light, she twisted off the gas cap and filled the tank, making sure nothing would block their escape. Then she secured the gas can to the rack behind the seat with a bungee cord, and put the key in the ignition, ready to go.

She peered through the crack in the open door at the hill behind the shed. No sign of Coop or the gunmen yet. Since she had time, she pulled out her grandfather's message and studied the symbols again: Selenium, carbon, gold. Hydrogen, chromium, chlorine.

She frowned, thinking hard. The elements didn't form a pattern. They weren't in their order on the periodic chart. But they had to mean something. Her grandfather had wanted her to figure this out.

And he was the most methodical person she knew. He didn't do anything by chance—unlike Coop. Coop lived for the excitement of the moment, did everything fast and hard. He was unpredictable, exhilarating, thrilling.

She pushed away that unruly thought, returning her mind to her grandfather's code. Each of the symbols had an atomic number. Selenium was thirty-four, carbon six, gold seventy-nine. And because this had to do with geo-caching… The first set might indicate latitude, the second longitude. The degrees wouldn't change—that would take her too far from the ghost town—but if those numbers represented minutes and seconds…

Her heart drumming, she dug through the backpack and retrieved the GPS. She checked her current position, then punched in the new coordinates and stilled. The cache was close by—only a hundred feet to the south, fifty yards to the west.

She widened the crack in the door and peeked out. Nothing moved on the hillside. She stepped outside, turned to survey the buildings to the west—the blacksmith's shop, the brothel, the stable…

Her heart skipped. *That was it*. The mine shaft in the stable. The one she'd fallen into as a kid—where she'd broken her arm. Her grandfather had nailed it shut for safety, even placed a bench on top, so few people knew it was there—except for her. And it was the perfect place to hide the cache.

She hesitated, knowing Coop would be furious if she left. But it wouldn't take long, only minutes. She could hurry over, grab the cache, and come right back.

Assuming those gunmen didn't kill her first.

She pressed her palms to her thighs. It seemed a terrible risk to take, even foolhardy, with those assassins prowling the hills. But she needed that flash drive to rescue her grandfather and prove his innocence—and her own.

Weathering the scandal about her parents had been hard enough. She'd been fourteen when her world had exploded. In an instant, she'd lost her family, her place in society, and had become a pariah to all her friends. Everyone thought her parents were traitors. People had taunted her, shunned her, harassed her. She'd spent years trying to prove her family's innocence, fighting the unfair rumors and lies.

Her grandfather had suffered, too. He'd lost important contracts at work, nearly gotten fired from his job. And neither of them would survive another scandal that bad. She had to put a halt to these new rumors and prove their innocence. She owed it to her parents, her grandfather, herself.

Her mind made up, she closed the door of the shed to hide the ATV. Sparrows chirped from a nearby rooftop. A jackrabbit bounded through the brush. She slid the backpack over her shoulder, screwed up her courage, then dashed to the building next door.

She stopped behind it and gasped for breath. Ignoring the pain battering her ankle, she tiptoed to the corner of the building and checked the road. Still nothing. She raced to the next building over and stopped again.

Knowing she couldn't waste precious time, she double-checked the coordinates on the GPS. But she had no doubt. The cache was in the stable. And she only had a few yards to go.

She cast another nervous glance at the hillside, then darted to the stable and slipped inside. She quickly moved away from the doorway and scanned the row of wooden stalls. Beer cans littered the ground. Leather bridles rotted on pegs. The hayloft door hung open above her, tapping rhythmically in the breeze.

She waited for another moment to make sure she was alone. A pigeon cooed and fluttered above her. The hayloft door kept banging, heightening her unease. She crept down the aisle, her nerves jittery, her head swiveling from stall to stall.

And then she spotted a man—lying prone on the ground.

She halted abruptly, her hands suddenly clammy, the hair on her arms erect. If that was Coop…

Panic seized her. She forced herself to step forward, her gaze fastened on the unmoving boots.

Then an arm shot out, grabbing her from behind. She slammed back against a hard chest. She instantly sprang into action, twisting, jabbing her elbow back, but couldn't shake him loose.

He tightened his arm under her rib cage and clamped his other hand over her mouth. Unable to breathe, desperate to get free, she stomped down hard on his foot.

"Damn it, Zoe. It's me," he rasped.

Coop. She stopped, sagged in his arms. Relief billowed through her, weakening her knees.

"Be quiet," he warned, his breath warm on her ear.

She nodded, and he relaxed his hold. She staggered away, then collapsed against the stall, trying to slow her rocketing pulse.

She turned back, met his eyes burning black with anger, the forbidding slash of his mouth. He'd acquired more weapons, and had a rifle slung over one shoulder, another pistol tucked into the waistband of his jeans. He looked lethal, as dangerous as their attackers, and an unsettled feeling slid up her spine.

And more doubts whispered inside her. Exactly how well did she know this man?

"I told you to stay put," he gritted out.

"But I know where the flash drive is."

"And I told you we don't have time. They've blocked the road to town." He nodded to the man lying on the floor. "I found him outside, heading for the shed. And he's commed up—he's got a radio. When he doesn't answer, the others will come to check."

Her stomach lurched. "Is…is he dead?"

"Unconscious. But not for long. We've got to get out before he comes to."

"Who is he?"

"I was trying to find that out when you showed up."

He strode back to the man and dropped to one knee.

Then he searched the gunman's back pockets, rolled him over, and did the same to the front. "No wallet."

He rose, pulled a cell phone from his pocket, and turned it on.

She blinked at the phone in his hands. "That's my phone."

"Yeah."

"But where—"

"Later."

Stunned, wondering why he hadn't told her he'd found her phone, she watched him photograph the man. Coop was right; this wasn't the time for questions.

But she wasn't going to let the subject drop.

He stuffed her phone back into his pocket, then tilted his head toward the door. "Come on. Let's get out of here."

But how? If those men had the road blocked...

She hesitated, searching her memory of the terrain. Aside from the sole road cutting through town, the only way out was over the mountain, the way they'd come. Unless...

"Wait. There's a mine shaft in the back of the stable— the one I fell into." Where her grandfather had hidden the flash drive. "It might lead us out."

"Show me."

She nodded, hurried past the remaining stalls. "It's right there, under the bench. He nailed one end down."

Coop made his way to the bench, then grabbed the end and pulled. He stopped, studied the ground, shifted position and tried again. His biceps bulged under the sleeves of his T-shirt. The hollows of his cheeks turned taut.

The bench creaked, then rose, pulling open a small trap door. Zoe bent over the hole and peered inside.

A wooden ladder led into the tunnel. "This is new. He must have installed this when he hid the flash drive."

Still holding up the bench, Coop spared her a glance. "You have the flashlight?"

She dug the flashlight out of the backpack and turned it on. "I'll go first." That way, if anything happened, Coop could pull her out.

She scooted over the opening and started down. The air grew cooler, mustier, as she descended. The dank, stone walls of the tunnel appeared.

But then a deep, male voice reached her ears—coming from the stable above.

She froze, whipped her gaze up to Coop. He jabbed down his thumb, motioning for her to continue into the tunnel, and she rushed down the remaining rungs.

He flew down the ladder behind her, balancing the trapdoor with one arm. She waited, her heart pounding fast and hard, praying their pursuers wouldn't catch up. Coop shut the door without a sound.

Shivering, she aimed the flashlight into the darkness—over the crudely chiseled walls, the low ceiling shored up by timber planks, the duffel bag propped by the wall.

"Coop, look," she whispered.

He strode over, opened the bag, and pulled out a carbine rifle. And her world spun even more. Since when did her grandfather own guns?

Coop lowered himself to one knee, then removed the contents of the bag—batteries, another flashlight, several magazines for the gun. Then he reached in and pulled out a plastic pine cone.

The cache.

Her pulse quickening, she propped the flashlight on the ground and took the cache from his hand. She unscrewed the top—and there it was. The missing flash drive.

So small, so innocent, so deadly.

She took it out and slid it into her pocket, just as a voice sounded directly above. Her lungs closed up. Ice invaded her veins.

And a deep sense of dread settled inside her. This tunnel had better lead out of the mountain.

Because if it didn't, they were trapped.

Chapter 8

Coop had to hand it to Zoe. She didn't crumple under pressure, didn't give up, even with trained killers dogging their heels.

He led the way down another dank tunnel inside the gold mine, his fingers stiff with cold, his stooped back screaming from the hours he'd spent hunched over, the duffel bag he was lugging banging against the stones.

By rights she should be done in. She'd been shot at, hiked all night without sleeping, had no more water or food. They'd spent hours wandering underground, scaling steep, precarious ladders, crawling through rubble-choked tunnels, coughing in the decades-old dust—and still hadn't found a way out.

And yet, Zoe hadn't panicked, hadn't once asked to rest, had even tried to conceal her exhaustion from him.

He paused and turned sideways in the cramped space, angling the flashlight to aid her steps. She limped toward him, her face as black as a miner's, her eyes reflecting her misery, her tattered clothes covered with dirt.

"I'm fine," she wheezed, anticipating his question.

"Right." He shook his head and continued hiking through the musty tunnel, the stale air cold on his arms. She amazed him, all right—and that was the problem. He didn't want to care about her. He didn't even want to like her, but he couldn't help it. She affected something deep inside him, evoking all sorts of unwanted emotions— admiration, tenderness, *regret.*

The truth was, somewhere along the line, he'd come to believe her. Maybe it was the risks she'd taken to find that flash drive. Or maybe it was the deep well of hurt he'd seen in her eyes when she'd learned her grandfather had betrayed her trust.

But he knew she wasn't faking that loyalty, that staunch dedication to her family. She didn't have it in her to lie.

And eight years ago, she hadn't tried to destroy *him.*

He exhaled, unable to deny the truth. Shaw had manipulated her back then—just as Coop was misleading her now. He had to tell her about his surveillance case. He couldn't keep putting it off. The longer he waited, the worse his deception would sting.

But not now. Not while they were trapped in this gold mine. He'd confess his guilt when he was sure that she'd be safe.

He rounded a bend, and the tunnel ended at the bottom of another shaft. He aimed the dwindling flashlight beam up the ladder bolted into the bedrock, and stifled a groan. Another climb to nowhere—just what they didn't need.

Zoe straggled to a stop beside him. "Again?" Her voice echoed his dismay.

"At least we're still going up." He just hoped they weren't

traveling in circles. The GPS didn't work underground, so he couldn't tell. "I'll go first."

He stuck the flashlight into his back pocket, adjusted the duffel bag on his shoulder, and started to climb. Half the rungs on the ladder were missing, the rest wobbly, and he feared that they would collapse. But he made it safely to the top, hoisted himself from the shaft, and shined the flashlight around the room.

Dynamite boxes littered the ground. More tunnels branched out from the cavern like spokes. Would this damned mine never end?

He wiped the dirt from his eyes onto his sleeve, then crouched at the top of the shaft. "Come on up," he called to Zoe.

He waited, angling the flashlight to aid her climb as she inched her way to the top. Her breath sawed in the echoing silence. Her hands trembled as she reached for the wooden rungs. When her head came into view, he grabbed her arm and hauled her the remaining way out. She stumbled to her feet beside him and swayed.

"We'll rest here for a minute," he decided.

"I can keep going."

"Humor me." He pulled her to a boulder near the wall, then dropped the duffel bag and stretched. He lowered himself to the rock, and Zoe settled beside him, her slender shoulder touching his. She shivered in the frigid air.

"You want my shirt?" he asked.

"No, I'm okay." She turned toward him, and in the dim beam from the flashlight he could see the anxiety haunting her eyes. "It's just…do you think we're lost?"

"No." He made his voice firm. "We've reached the main level. We'll be out soon." *He hoped.*

"That's good." She wiped her brow on the hem of her

blouse. "Once we're out I need to find a computer so I can see what's on that flash drive."

"We'll head to a town, find a motel. We can rest, eat, shower, make plans."

She let out a wistful sigh. "A shower sounds wonderful. I don't think I've ever been this filthy."

She'd definitely seen better days. Dirt coated her skin. Her once-prim blouse barely hung by a thread. Her shorts were torn clear up her thigh.

His gaze slid from her legs to her lips. Even dirty, she made his pulse race. And he could think of far more interesting things to do in a motel room than sleep.

Forcing his mind off that dangerous track, he swept the flashlight around the room—over an old wooden spool, a forgotten barrel of carbide, a pile of discarded boards. He considered turning off the light to preserve the batteries, but decided against it. The silence in the mine was unnerving enough.

"You never said why you have my cell phone," Zoe said.

Coop nodded, knowing he should tell her about his job right now. She'd provided the perfect opening to set things straight. "I found it in the plane. I should have given it to you then, but I..."

His gaze met hers, and the vulnerability in her eyes halted his words. He couldn't do it. He couldn't shatter her illusions. Not here. Not yet.

"...I forgot," he lied. "But I'm glad we had it. At least we've got a photo of one of the men now."

She nodded, her eyebrows gathering, but she appeared to accept his excuse. "Do you think they know we're in the mine?"

That was the million-dollar question. "I doubt it. They're probably still searching the ghost town."

"How many men were there?"

"Three that I could see. The one I'd dragged into the stable, two more blocking the road down the hill." But they'd been heavily armed, even had military-grade night NODs—night observation devices—leading him to wonder who was funding this gig. "They were speaking Arabic," he added.

"Arabic?" Her eyes flew to his. "Are you sure?"

He nodded. "I learned a few words in the Persian Gulf. Enough to recognize the language."

"You mean…they could be terrorists? Like al-Qaeda?" Her voice squeaked.

"Or someone like them."

"But…" She pressed her fingers to her lips. "Why would terrorists target my grandfather? How did they know about his work?"

"He's pretty famous. Maybe they caught wind of his research, offered to buy the information from him, and he agreed."

"He would never do that."

"You don't know that. He might have needed the money. Or maybe he sympathized with their beliefs."

She shook her head, causing dirt to fall from her hair. "He doesn't care about money. I told you that. And he doesn't pay any attention to politics, unless it affects funding for his work. Plus, he was kidnapped. That proves he wasn't involved."

"He took that flash drive from the lab."

"Because he wanted to protect his work, not sell it. I know you don't believe it, but my grandfather's not a traitor, Coop."

She was right. He didn't believe it. But he'd never convince her without proof. "Fine. Let's assume it wasn't him. Who else had access to his work?"

"It's hard to say. I told you his work is classified, SCI."

Sensitive Compartmented Information. He knew the system. "So different people have access to different pieces of the work."

She dipped her head. "Not many can see the entire project. Even after it's done, it stays secret. The government might downgrade it at some point, declassify it, but that could be years down the road."

Coop mulled that over, the doubts that had been lurking in the periphery of his mind coming back full force. "So you think someone else is the traitor and he was framed?"

"Yes."

"But it's quite a coincidence, isn't it, your family being targeted twice?"

"Just the opposite. We're the perfect people to frame. Everyone still believes my parents were spies, so shouldn't we be, too?"

Unless there really was a link. "So tell me about your parents."

Her startled gaze swung to his. "You think the cases could be connected?"

"I don't think we can rule it out."

Her brows gathered into a frown. "Well, they worked with my grandfather. My father was a physicist, my mother a chemist, like I am. She was brilliant."

The bitter edge to her tone surprised him. "You're smart."

"Maybe. But she set a high standard. And I guess… My grandfather always gave me the impression I didn't quite measure up."

Coop had grown up with the opposite problem. Everyone in his town had thought he was destined for ruin. Even he'd believed it, until Pedro had given him something to live for, a reason to change. "Is that why you became a chemist?"

"Partly. I liked science… And after my parents died, I felt I owed it to them, that I had to prove that we weren't crooks.

"I was fourteen when it happened," she continued. "I don't know the details of the case. It was classified information, highly sensitive. But everyone thought we were traitors. We became pariahs overnight. People stared at us wherever we went, shouted things. We got hate mail, nasty phone calls—even death threats. Someone shot up our house."

His sympathy surged. Even he hadn't suffered that much. "They died in an accident, right?"

"Hit-and-run. They were coming home from a meeting with their lawyer. Nothing was ever proven about the espionage, but everyone assumed they'd done it. And they weren't around to defend themselves."

He hesitated, not wanting to hurt her feelings, but he had to ask. "Is there any chance it was true?"

"No. I've thought about it a lot, especially lately, but they were framed. They had to be. But…"

"But what?"

She didn't answer right away. She brushed some dirt from her shorts, her expression troubled. "It was probably nothing. I might have misunderstood. But they'd been arguing a lot before they died. They'd stop when I came into the room, but I could tell. You know how you can feel that tension? And later I wondered…"

She shook her head. "But they couldn't have been spies. What did they have to gain? They never traveled to foreign countries, didn't live a lavish lifestyle. No secret bank account came to light. I'm sure they were framed, Coop.

"And now it's happening again. This time to my grandfather and me."

He picked up her hand, cradled it in his own, his protective instincts winging back. "Don't worry. We'll figure this out."

"I know." Her mouth wobbled. "But you believe me, don't you? That we aren't spies?"

The stricken note in her voice made his heart roll. "I know you're not a spy," he said carefully, making no claim about Shaw. He squeezed her hand, caressed her cool skin with his thumb. And that deep sense of certainty settled inside him. He did know Zoe. She was honorable, trustworthy. The most loyal person he knew.

So why had he doubted her that summer? He'd known she wouldn't have lied. And she never would have had her grandfather do her dirty work. She would have told him directly if she didn't want him around.

She was more honest than he was. He still hadn't told her why he was here.

More guilt pounded through him like storm waves eroding a cliff. He couldn't keep putting it off. The longer he waited, the harder she'd take the news.

"Thank you for believing me and helping me," she whispered. She squeezed his hand, and his stomach wrenched even more. "I don't know what I'd have done without you, and I…I'm glad you're here."

He gazed into her trusting eyes, feeling like a total heel, his conscience screaming at him to come clean.

He ran his hand down his face and looked away, knowing he had to tell her now. He should just blurt it out, admit everything—and not worry about how she felt.

But he couldn't do it. And it wasn't only because he hated to hurt her, although that was a major part. There was something different about Zoe. Ever since he'd met her, she'd made him think about his life, made him want to succeed—to be a better man than he was.

And damned if he could stand to let her down.

He rose, angry at her for trusting him, even more furious at himself. "Come on. Let's get out of this mine before our light runs out."

But as he tramped through the nearest tunnel, he knew he couldn't outrun his conscience. He had to tell her the truth.

And he had to do it soon.

Zoe crawled through the tunnel behind Coop an hour later, heedless of the stones gouging her knees and palms, her gaze locked on a sliver of light. After hours trapped in the oppressive darkness, wandering through silent, tomblike tunnels and nearly getting crushed by debris, they'd finally found their way out.

Coop pushed through a clump of branches blocking the exit, then reached back and gripped her hand. She staggered to her feet, sharp twigs jabbing her face and legs, so ecstatic she wanted to weep.

What an ordeal! Hunger gnawed a hole in her gut. Her head reeled like a washing machine set to spin. She closed her eyes and filled her lungs with warm, sweet air, wanting to kiss the sun-drenched earth.

She'd been so scared, so afraid they'd be buried in the blackness, condemned to die in that echoing gloom…

But they weren't out of danger yet.

She blinked rapidly in the blinding sunlight, knowing she couldn't afford to relax. Their pursuers were still out there, searching the mountain nearby.

"Any idea where we are?" she asked, glancing around.

"The north side of the mountain, I think. Do you still have the GPS?"

She reached into the backpack and pulled it out, keeping her gaze on Coop as he turned it on. Dirt speckled his shoulders and hair. Heavy stubble darkened the contours of his face. A rifle peeked from the duffel bag he carried, adding to his dangerous look.

She grimaced at the injustice. He grew sexier as time wore on, while she looked as if she'd rolled in mud.

He glanced up and motioned toward a parched hill. "There should be a campground over that hill, about two miles away, a staging area for backcountry hikers."

"You think we can bum a ride?"

"We'd better not. We can't risk being seen. We don't know if we're in the news. And the fewer innocent people we involve in this, the better."

She agreed, especially with those possible terrorists at large. But the thought of crossing the desert on foot made her want to cry. "Then why go to the campground?"

"I'm going to borrow a car."

"Borrow? You mean steal one?"

His dark brow rose. "Unless you've got a better idea."

She gaped at him for a moment, then let out a strangled laugh, not sure which shocked her more—how completely she trusted Coop, or how little it bothered her to break the law. She—the same woman who'd once driven ten miles to return a dollar a grocery store clerk had over-reimbursed—was now fleeing the police, had nuclear secrets hidden in her pocket, was about to commit a felony with nary a qualm.

Funny how morality changed with her life at stake.

She shrugged and tossed her scruples to the desert wind. "All right, Clyde. Let's go steal ourselves a car."

* * *

They found a truck, a dilapidated old pickup that Coop quickly hot-wired, testimony to his misspent youth. Zoe climbed inside, buckled her seat belt, and promptly fell asleep, waking only when the truck came to a stop hours later in a tiny town.

She rubbed her gritty eyes, her mind still fuzzy with sleep, and glanced around. They'd pulled up to a peeling, one-story motel on the two-lane highway through town. There was a gas station on one side of the motel, a combination casino/cafe on the other. She saw a stop light down the road, a boarded-up garage next to an agricultural supply store, a few deserted side streets baking in the midday heat.

"Where are we?" The hot breeze blew through the open windows, spawning a dust devil near the truck.

"Lizard Point." Coop set the parking brake but left the engine running. "Stay here. I'm going to see about a room."

"I'll come with you."

He hesitated. His gaze traveled from her face to her feet and back up. "You'd better not."

"I look that bad?"

He swiped his finger down the bridge of her nose, the gentle touch making her breath catch. He lifted his blackened finger and quirked a brow.

She winced. "I'll stay here."

"Good decision." His quick grin crinkled his eyes. He jumped out of the truck and made his way toward the motel's office, closing the distance with easy strides. When he disappeared into the building, she undid her seat belt and looked in the rearview mirror.

She shrieked. Her face was black with grime. Her hair

had become a rat's nest, adorned with dirt and twigs. Her arms and legs were covered with filth, her clothes mere rags, as if she'd barely survived a bomb blast.

And she felt even worse. A terrible thirst clawed her throat. Her stomach was so hollow she could hardly think. Every muscle protested the tumble off that cliff, and she wanted desperately to sleep.

Coop emerged from the office a second later. He leaped back into the idling truck, released the brake, and shot her a grin. "We're in luck. Room thirty-eight. Around the back."

"Did you have to show an ID?"

"No, I paid cash. They preferred it. I got the feeling their clientele isn't the best."

"I'm just glad we got a room." And that Coop had money—because her wallet was in her knapsack in that ravine.

They bumped through the rutted parking lot to the back of the motel. The numbers had fallen off the door, but she could see thirty-eight outlined in the faded paint, the second room to the end. The room had a Dumpster view, its curtains half hanging off the rod. The bottom of the door looked gnawed, as if a rodent had feasted on the wood.

Or someone had kicked it in. Apprehensive, she glanced around the deserted parking lot.

Coop grimaced. "Sorry it's not nicer."

She was touched that he cared. "Don't be silly. As long as it has a shower and a bed, I don't mind."

She climbed out of the truck and went to the door, taking her grandfather's backpack with her. Coop jiggled the key in the flimsy lock. "Not much security."

"We don't have anything to steal."

"Except that flash drive."

She shivered at the grim reminder and patted her pocket where the flash drive was. It was hard to believe people would kill for something so small, so ordinary. And as soon as she got to a computer, she'd find out why.

Coop pushed open the door, and she limped ahead of him into the room. A bare lightbulb hung from the ceiling. The odor of stale cigarette smoke permeated the air. A sagging double bed with a dingy, Southwestern-styled bedspread took up most of the space.

Coop closed the door and turned on the light. "I told him I was alone," he said, sounding apologetic.

"That was smart, safer." She eyed the stained red carpet, the television bolted to the wall, the locked door to the adjoining room.

The far too narrow bed.

The room grew hot. She clutched her hands, feeling suddenly awkward. And suddenly, the memory of that kiss rushed back—Coop's erotic mouth, the warm, male scent of his skin. The thrilling bulge nudging the apex of her thighs…

She struggled to sound offhand. "This is the first time in almost two days we haven't been moving."

"Yeah." He speared his hand through his hair, dislodging dirt and making his biceps flex. His gaze collided with hers, then shifted away, leaving a blast of heat in its wake. "You want to shower first?"

"No, go ahead."

He slanted his head. "It won't take long. Then I'll go scrounge up supplies."

"All right."

He squeezed past the bed, his arm brushing hers, and every cell inside her sprang to life. He entered the bathroom and closed the door, and she tried to get a grip.

She was acting ridiculous. Certainly they could share a room without thinking about sex.

Right.

She grabbed the complimentary bottle of water and gulped it down, not bothering with the plastic cup. Determined to focus on their predicament instead of the virile man stripping off his clothes behind that door, she turned the television to the news. Then she sat on the edge of the bed, and peeled off her shoes and socks. She had blisters on one heel. Her twisted ankle throbbed, but an ACE bandage would remedy that.

The news channel cut to sports. Still trying not to think about Coop, she took another long pull of water and stared at the men playing baseball on the screen. It seemed unreal that the world had continued on its normal course while her life had fallen apart.

And then the shower turned on, and every one of her nerve endings went berserk. She tried not to imagine Coop standing in the shower naked—his thick, black hair slicked to his head, his hard muscles glistening under the spray, water sluicing down his shoulders…down the roped tendons of his arms, down his flat abdomen to parts below… She closed her eyes and groaned.

How on earth were they going to lie together in that bed? The room didn't have a couch, just a small, rickety armchair in the corner. And she wouldn't let an animal sleep on the filthy floor.

She sighed and realized she might as well admit it. She wanted to have sex with Coop. She hungered for that excitement, to relive the pleasure of his arms.

And was that so wrong? Was it selfish to want to escape reality for awhile, to forget the danger, the terrible fear, and surrender to the mind-numbing bliss?

She didn't know. Maybe it *was* selfish. But more than

guilt and the urgent need to find her grandfather held her back. She'd never been the type to engage in casual sex. And she was already dangerously close to falling for Coop. Memories of the past kept rushing back, merging with the reality of the man he'd become—a brave, strong man she craved and admired. Could she spend a night in his arms and stay detached?

The shower turned off. She jumped to her feet, sat back down, then bolted upright again, clutching the water bottle to her chest. She heard the rustle of clothes, and then the bathroom door jerked open, discharging a billow of steam.

Coop stepped out. He wore the same clothes—jeans, T-shirt, flight boots. But his hair was wet, his T-shirt clinging to his broad chest. Drops of water trickled through the whiskers on his face, turning the neck of his T-shirt damp.

Their gazes connected. Her nerves went into overdrive, jittering with sudden heat. His sexual appeal hit her like a desert sandstorm, shutting down all rational thought. She yearned to touch him so badly she had to clench her hands to resist.

The moment stretched. She knew she should look away, get a grip, move so he could get by. But the heat in his gaze and the tension pulsing between them held her in place. He wanted her. She couldn't mistake the raw, simmering hunger in his granite eyes.

And she knew right then that she wouldn't resist.

"Be careful out there," she croaked.

He nodded, releasing her gaze, and she managed to step aside. "Lock the door," he said, his voice rough. "I'll take the key. Don't open to anyone else."

"I won't." But as he headed for the door, his muscles

rippling, his raw sexuality like a kick to her throat, she had a feeling the real danger wouldn't come from without.

But the devastation this man could wreak on her heart.

Chapter 9

Coop thought that safeguarding Zoe had been hard, but protecting her from himself was going to do him in.

Gripping the bag of supplies he'd bought at the café next door, he unlocked the door to the motel room and strode inside. He didn't know how he would survive the next few hours. Her gentle touch, the blatant hunger in her eyes had nearly brought him to his knees. How could he lie beside her on that bed?

He shouldn't touch her; he realized that. She was scared right now, worried about her grandfather. Their assailants could catch them unaware. No matter how strong the temptation, he had to resist.

Even if they were alone in a too-small motel room in an even smaller bed.

He pulled one of the T-shirts he bought from the plastic bag and tossed it on the chair. Then, steeling himself, he knocked on the bathroom door.

"Just a minute," she called, her voice muffled.

He waited, trying not to envision her naked, the muscles of his shoulders tense. She opened the door a crack, letting steam escape, and peeked out. Her hair was wet, her eyelashes spiky and moist, the scrape visible on her freshly scrubbed face. Water trickled down her cheek, gathering at the base of her throat.

And he couldn't stop his gaze from devouring every alluring inch he could see of her—her bare shoulders pink from the sun, the cleavage visible above the towel she gripped, her long, slender thighs and bare feet.

He dragged his gaze back up with effort and cleared the huskiness from his throat. "I got you a T-shirt." He handed her the plastic bag. "There wasn't much of a selection." Just a few touristy items on a rack in the café.

She tugged the shirt from the bag. It had a silhouette of Nevada in blue on the front, flanked by various state symbols—a mountain bluebird, a desert tortoise, a bristlecone pine tree.

A smile lit her eyes. She held the shirt to her nose and inhaled, as if smelling the finest perfume. "This is great. It's so clean."

And she looked too appealing.

"There's more stuff in the bag. Toothbrushes, a bandage for your ankle." Shaving supplies for himself.

"A toothbrush?" Her smile broadened, her eyes dancing with delight. "That's better than diamonds."

She opened the door wider. Then her arms came around him, bombarding him with sensations—full breasts, warm, naked arms, the shampoo scent of her hair. But just as quickly, she whirled around, slipped back into the bathroom, and shut the door.

He forced himself to breathe.

She was going to kill him, all right.

His pulse thundering, he paced back to the television and turned it on, keeping the volume low. He tried not to think about Zoe dropping the towel, pulling that T-shirt over her breasts, the feel of her satiny skin…

He peeled off his own filthy T-shirt and donned the one he'd bought for himself. He heard Zoe rustling in the bathroom, the faucet turning on, then off. He sat on the edge of the bed, stared unseeing at the television, way too conscious of how her bare legs had brushed against his, the arousing feel of her curves.

He could push this. It wouldn't take much to get her to agree; he'd seen the desire in her eyes, felt her response to his kiss. And God knew he was willing; he'd been deployed for months, then spent several lonely weeks sitting at Pedro's airstrip after that.

And with anyone else he wouldn't hesitate. But this was Zoe. Nothing about her had ever been casual. And he couldn't take advantage of her now. He had to exert some self-control, do the right thing.

Be the honorable man she believed him to be.

No matter how hot they'd once burned.

He scowled at the television, his attention briefly diverted by people picketing in Las Vegas, protesting the new nuclear power plant going online in a couple of days. He turned up the volume, wondering if it had anything to do with Zoe's grandfather, although he didn't see how.

Then the news went to a commercial, Zoe emerged from the bathroom, and he flicked off the television. He rose, tossed the remote aside and turned to face her. She paused a few feet away.

And before he could stop it, his gaze swept the length of her, over her lightly freckled nose, the tiny mole by her wide mouth, the loose fall of her wet, blonde hair. The T-shirt dwarfed her, nearly covering her shorts, but couldn't disguise the fullness of her breasts. Her legs and feet were bare, making her look softer, more approachable.

More tempting.

"You look clean."

Her lips curved, a wry smile warming her eyes. "I washed my hair about ten times. I used up all the shampoo." Her gaze dropped to his T-shirt, and her eyes warmed even more. "Great shirt."

The edge of his mouth ticked up. His shirt was black with "I love Nevada" printed across the front. "It was the only other choice. I didn't think we'd want to match."

She tilted her head. "Well, if we have to pose as tourists, at least we're clean ones."

"Yeah." He lifted his hand, tested the heavy growth of beard stubble along his jaw. "But if you can hold off on food for a minute, I'd better shave. I don't want to scare little children."

"Good idea." She leaned close, ran her fingers lightly over his face, spurring a surge of heat in his blood.

And he couldn't help but react. He caught her wrist, trapping her palm against his face, pinning her in place with his eyes.

His heart tapped an irregular beat. For an eternity, neither moved. And the desire to haul her into his arms and slake the fierce need building inside him laid siege to his resolve.

She wanted him. He saw it her eyes, felt her pulse scatter under his thumb like a panicked jackrabbit zigzagging through the brush.

And a litany of warnings blared in his mind. They didn't have time. He couldn't complicate things. Zoe wasn't the type for a simple affair.

He dropped his hand and forced himself to squeeze past her. The disappointment in her eyes almost made him cave. But he strode into the bathroom and kicked shut the door, then braced his hands on the sink. He hung his head, summoning every ounce of willpower he had to keep from jerking that door open again.

He'd done the right thing. He'd had to keep his hands off her. But like a man facing a firing squad, he knew the reprieve wouldn't last. This attraction was growing too strong.

And next time, he wouldn't have the power to resist.

The torture continued as Coop sat across from Zoe at the café a short time later, their knees bumping in the cramped booth, her clean, feminine scent taunting his nerves.

"That was the best hamburger I've ever eaten," she announced. She picked up her last French fry and munched it down. "And the fastest. I think I just set a speed-eating record."

"Yeah, hunger will do that." He'd wolfed down two burgers himself. But even the desperate need for food didn't match the lust quickly demolishing his control. He eyed the soft lilt to her mouth, the glorious blond silk tumbling around her face—and he wanted to fist that hair in his hands, pull her naked beneath him, make her eyes grow glazed with desire.

He clenched his teeth, fighting the heavy rush pulsing inside him, and lowered his gaze to her empty plate. "You want more?"

"No, I'm good for now. We'd better get to work."

"Good idea." He slapped some bills on the table and scanned the parking lot outside the café. No one had taken an interest in them so far. But there weren't many towns in the desert, not enough places to hide. And once their assailants realized they'd escaped…

"The computers are in the back by the restrooms," he said, keeping his voice low. "I'll stay by the slot machines and keep watch."

"All right."

She scooted across the bench seat, but he snagged her wrist and stopped her before she could rise. He waited until her gaze swung back to his. "Listen, Zoe. If anything happens and I have to leave, don't follow me. Climb out through the bathroom window and leave."

Protests gathered in her eyes, but he cut them off. "I mean it." He hated to scare her, but he had to keep her safe. "You've got to listen this time. Don't worry about me. I'll catch up with you later. Just get out of here and run."

"All right." When he didn't move, she lifted her brows. "I said I would do it."

"You'd better." He held on to her wrist for another heartbeat, and then let go. Her eyes flashing, she snatched back her arm and rose, then stalked past the slot machines to the back of the café.

He stayed in his seat, eyeing the other patrons to see if they watched her go. The waitress continued wiping down tables. A gray-haired couple sat at a nearby booth, their heads bent over a map. Two soldiers—out of uniform, but clearly marines with their high and tight haircuts—sat on stools at the counter, laughing and drinking beer.

Coop stood, then strolled over to the slot machines, choosing one with a view of the door. He pulled some quarters from his pocket and started to play, keeping an eye on the road outside.

But as the slot machine's tumbler spun, so did the questions in his mind. Why hadn't a search team returned to the crash site? How were those terrorists connected to Shaw—assuming that's what they were? And how were the kidnappers going to notify Zoe about the rendezvous point?

He tugged her cell phone from his pocket and turned it on. There were no missed calls, no new text messages. She'd wiped her call history clean.

And realization dawned. She'd lied to him. She already knew the drop-off point. She just hadn't revealed it to him.

His forehead furrowed, the awareness that she'd deceived him digging at his nerves. But he couldn't really blame her; in her place, he'd have done the same. Still, her distrust rankled, which was ironic given how he had lied to her.

Frowning over that thought, he pocketed the phone, surveyed the parking lot again, then scooped up his winnings and went after Zoe. He found her hunched over one of the two computers crammed against the back wall.

She glanced up absently as he approached. "I'm almost done."

She swiveled back to the computer, and he leaned over her shoulder, studying the complex equations on the screen. She scrolled through the data quickly, her hands tapping the keyboard, going through page after page.

And suddenly, his perception shifted. He'd always admired Zoe's intelligence, but seeing her whiz through the complicated formulas forced him to alter his view. The woman was more than smart; she was brilliant.

And that revelation spawned another—that eight years ago, he hadn't been fair to Zoe. He hadn't thought about what she'd needed, not really. He hadn't thought enough about her career, about where she'd need to live to do her research or what pursuing her goals might entail.

Too caught up in his own plans, he'd expected her to accommodate him.

Which didn't make him much better than Shaw.

That thought made him grimace, but he couldn't deny the truth. Shaw had pressured her to become a scientist. Coop had expected her to compromise her career to follow his.

Neither had thought of her.

She shut down the program and ejected the flash drive. For a moment she just sat there, the flash drive clenched in her fist. Then she pushed out her chair and stood up.

The hurt in her eyes jerked him out of his thoughts. "What is it? What happened?"

"He…" She shook her head, compressed her lips.

"Is it what you thought? Did he succeed?"

She inhaled audibly, as if pulling herself together, and the misery in her eyes tore at his heart. "I think so. I haven't looked at all the files yet. Some are encrypted, and it's going to take me some time to get in. But it's not just that. There's something else."

"What?"

"This material isn't his, Coop. Not all of it. He stole it."

Shaw had stolen the work? "How do you know?"

Her voice turned raw. "Because he stole it from me."

Zoe was still stunned when they entered their motel room minutes later. She didn't want to believe it. Her grandfather—the man she'd respected and revered—had stolen her work. He was a thief, a fraud, a common criminal!

She sank onto the edge of the bed, numb from the discovery, and rested her head in her hands. All these years she'd admired him, following his guidance and advice—while he'd been living a lie.

Coop stopped beside the television set, put down the weapons he'd brought in from the truck, and pulled the small chair close to the bed. Then he dropped into the chair and braced his forearms on his knees. "All right. Start at the beginning and tell me what you found."

She inhaled to marshal her thoughts. "When I was in graduate school, I had an idea. I thought I could separate the uranium isotopes in transuranic waste—a nuclear by-product—by using reverse osmosis. I thought for sure it would work. I told my grandfather about it, thinking he could help me. I even suggested a proprietary membrane we could use. But he told me it wouldn't work, that he'd already tried something similar and failed. He convinced me to pursue something else.

"But he stole my idea. He used it as the basis of his work. He lied to me and betrayed my trust."

Coop nodded, but a shadow darkened his eyes. "Let's get back to that part in a minute. First off, does the process work?"

"I think so." She dragged in another breath, feeling flayed inside but trying to focus on what mattered most. "I didn't check all the subfiles…they're encrypted and I didn't have time. But if the summary he wrote is accurate, he used multiple chains of membranes—exactly how I suggested—to extract the uranium. Then he reprocessed it into weapons-grade material."

No wonder he'd risked everything to save that research. The invention would rock the world, revolutionize technology. But the destruction it could cause in the wrong hands…

A deep feeling of foreboding pricked her nerves.

And to think she'd had a part in it—however unwilling she'd been.

Coop grimaced. "I'm still a step behind you. Assuming those men chasing us are terrorists, exactly why would they want this procedure?"

"They could make nuclear bombs. Easily. They wouldn't need expensive equipment, just a small amount of nuclear waste."

"That can't be easy to get."

"No, but it's not impossible. The dumps aren't as well guarded as they should be. There have been warnings about that for years. And you'd be surprised how much radioactive material goes missing. It's not publicized; they don't want to scare the public. And usually it's just a mistake, something innocent, like a mix-up at a lab. But it happens more than you'd think. And then there's the foreign black market, like material coming out of the former Soviet Union. That's a major international concern."

"So why don't more criminals make nuclear bombs?"

She spread her hands. "Well, obviously, you need the technology. And transporting radioactive material is dangerous. You need special protection, all sorts of safeguards to keep from getting poisoned. But…"

"But what?"

"If someone is prepared to die, like a suicide bomber, he wouldn't worry about the protection much."

Coop's dark brows knitted together. "I still don't get it. If they manage to get the waste, why bother with this procedure? Why not just spread it around in a dirty bomb?"

"Because a dirty bomb isn't as dangerous as people think. It's bad—don't get me wrong. It would contaminate the area and cause deaths, and create a lot of fear, but the radiation exposure wouldn't be that widespread.

"But this…" She couldn't keep the dread from her voice. "This would be enormous, shocking, a nuclear bomb complete with a mushroom cloud."

Her belly fisted tight, the enormity of it all sinking in. She touched the flash drive in her pocket, conscious of the information it contained, the terrible responsibility she now held in her hands.

"I saw something on the news earlier," Coop said slowly. "About that new nuclear power plant in Vegas. Could they get the material from there?"

"No. They'd never get at the nuclear material directly. There are too many safeguards in place. But if they already had some material and used this bomb on the nuclear plant…"

She felt the blood leach from her face. It would be catastrophic. The worst explosion since Hiroshima and Nagasaki in World War II.

And the opening of that nuclear power plant was a high-profile event. Even the president was supposed to attend. It would grab the attention of the world.

"Dear God," she whispered. She pressed her hand to her throat, trembling from the horror the idea evoked. "Do you think…?"

Coop rose, then paced across the small room to the door and back. Then he sat beside her on the bed. "We can't jump to conclusions. We don't know that they have any nuclear waste. We don't even know who's involved in this, whether they're terrorists or not. All we've got is that guy's photo we took in the ghost town. And whoever kidnapped Shaw can't have the formula yet if it's on that flash drive. So as far as we know, they can't do anything bad."

Unless her grandfather had been tortured, made to replicate his work. But then why were armed men pursuing her?

She shook her head and tried to think through the burgeoning fear. "I can't let anyone get this. I don't care if it's government property or not. It's too dangerous. The world doesn't need a way to make weapons like this." Especially terrorists.

But if she didn't pay the ransom, her grandfather would die.

She swallowed and tried to think. She didn't want to help her grandfather. He'd stolen her ideas and destroyed her trust. But he still didn't deserve to lose his life.

So what on earth should she do?

"How much time do we have?" Coop asked.

"Not much." She glanced at her watch. "Nine hours."

"Where's the rendezvous point?"

She hesitated, but his gaze didn't waver from hers. "The truth, Zoe."

She sighed. There was no point hiding it now. "The Mesquite Wildlife Preserve at midnight. At the old ranch house."

He nodded. "Then here's what we'll do. We'll rest for an hour and let this sink in. Then we'll decide on a plan."

"But—"

"You're dead on your feet, Zoe. You're not going to help your grandfather if you collapse."

Coop was right. She was too exhausted to think straight, and she had no idea what to do. Her grandfather had told her not to trust anyone—not the Navy, not the police or FBI. But he'd led a secret life, stolen her work. And now she couldn't trust *him*.

She kneaded the ache throbbing between her brows, struggled to put those thoughts aside. But her mind kept spinning around, more doubts tumbling through. "I never would have believed it before, but if he stole my work… What else did he do? Is he a traitor? Did he set up my parents, too?"

Had he killed his own child?

"You don't know that," Coop said quietly. He picked up her hand, threaded his fingers through hers.

"You're right." She exhaled, tried to calm down. She didn't have any facts right now and shouldn't imagine the worst. She squeezed Coop's hand, reassured by his warmth and strength.

But this revelation undermined her foundations, threatened everything she'd once believed—even who she was. She lifted her gaze to Coop's, giving voice to the fear. "But what if he is a traitor? What does that make me?"

Coop angled around to face her, tipped up her chin with his free hand. "It makes you the same loyal person you've always been."

Her heart softened. She managed a shaky smile, grateful he understood, glad she could trust him with this—and that he had agreed to help her after the damage her grandfather had done.

And she could no longer deny the truth. It was too obvious. Coop never would have dumped her, no matter what her parents had done, no matter how their actions affected his career. He would have stood by her, just as he supported her now.

"Coop…I'm so sorry," she said, her voice uneven. "I never should have doubted you."

He shifted his gaze away. "Forget it. It doesn't matter."

"It does to me." Because by trusting the wrong man she'd lost something real, something precious, something she could never regain.

Coop's love.

An unbearable ache lodged inside her, a yearning for all that she'd lost. Her throat burned with emotions—regret, sorrow, remorse.

She blinked, struggling to control the gut-wrenching feelings, the fierce need swelling inside. Turning, she met his gaze, letting him see her desire.

His eyes darkened. His face went taut. "You're tired. We both are. We need to rest."

"I need you," she whispered. She reached out, did what she'd craved to do all day. She ran her finger along his jaw line, smooth now from his recent shave, and traced the beard shadow under his skin. Then she curved her hand around his strong neck and tugged his face down to hers.

"Kiss me, Coop."

He rested his forehead against hers, their mouths nearly touching, his warm breath grazing her lips. "Damn it, Zoe." His voice came out rough. "I'm trying to do the right thing here."

"The right thing?" She let out a laugh. "I have no idea what that is anymore." Her life had been blasted apart, her security destroyed, everything she'd believed turned into a lie.

"All I know is what I want now." Comfort, oblivion. A chance to recapture what she'd thrown away, if only for this moment in time.

"You," she whispered. "I want you, Coop."

He swore, groaned in surrender, and she abandoned herself to the bliss.

Chapter 10

Never had anything so wrong felt so right.

Coop gave in to the kiss, his senses filled with Zoe's sweet scent, savoring the hot, moist silk of her mouth. He knew it was wrong to touch her. They were in danger. She was vulnerable right now. She deserved a better man than him.

But nothing had felt this good in years—the soft, sleek lure of her lips, the seductive velvet of her skin. He was lost, falling in deeper, riveted by her mouth, her taste, her feel.

Hunger pounded inside him, a sudden urgency he couldn't ignore. Zoe had always had this effect on him—instant, dizzying, electric. The instant he'd seen her—her blue eyes sparkling, that sex-goddess mole winking—he'd longed to strip off her conservative clothes, bare the erotic seductress beneath, and discover just how hot she burned.

His body tightened. His racing heart doubled its beat. Then Zoe speared her hands in his hair, making tiny moans at the back of her throat, erasing every thought from his head.

Except one—Zoe naked. Under him. Right now. He wanted to rip off her clothes, surrender to the reckless craving, take her hard and fast and deep.

But he had to slow down, make this good. A quick, torrid coupling would never be enough with Zoe. He wanted to make her eyes grow blurry and dazed. Make her hunger and tremble with want. Drive her past desire into desperation, making her need for him so urgent that she'd shake with it, cry for it, beg for him to make her his.

She made another helpless sound, digging her fingers into his shoulders, sending a jolt of heat through his veins. But he gentled the kiss, rained kisses down her jaw to the creamy skin of her throat.

Her pulse rioted beneath his mouth. Her ragged breath feathered his ear. She smelled like sin, tasted like every fantasy he'd ever had. He stroked his hands down her spine, palmed the curving flare of her hips, already losing control.

She had the most beautiful body he'd ever seen—long, slender legs, full, lush breasts. And he liked that she didn't flaunt it, that she disguised her explosive sexuality behind a modest facade. The demure clothes only heightened his anticipation, challenging him to imagine the woman beneath.

She let her head fall back with a moan, and relentless need hammered his blood. He laved the curve of her throat, plundered her mouth in a ravenous kiss, but it wasn't nearly enough. He wrenched himself away, tugged her T-shirt over her head, dropped his gaze to the modest bra molding her breasts.

His breath turned hoarse and fast. His blood rushed straight to his groin. Her nipples pebbled under his gaze, and he ran his finger along the vee of her cleavage, tracing the tempting valleys and curves.

Her eyes fluttered closed. Her body quivered under his touch, her lips parting on a breathless moan. And then he lowered his head, kissed her breasts through the fabric of her bra, worshiping her with his hands and lips and tongue.

She gripped his hair, holding him close, and hunger slammed through his veins. Veering beyond control, trembling with the need to feel her, he dropped back onto the bed. Then he pulled her atop him, pressing her hips to where he burned the most.

Tremors skipped inside him. He tightened his grip, keeping her locked in place, rocking instinctively against her heat. She leaned forward, and her hair fluttered around them, sheltering them like a curtain of silk. And his world narrowed to this one woman, this one moment in time.

Zoe. Brilliant. Loyal. Exciting.

Her lips were swollen and lush, her eyes limpid and dark, and his pulse pounded faster yet. Her thighs cupped his rigid length, detonating a firestorm of need in his blood, too urgent, too strong to resist.

He shuddered, his hands roaming her back, her waist, the round, ripe swells of her breasts. He wanted to forget going slowly, just strip off her remaining clothes and plunge into her blissful warmth, reliving the tight, pulsing feel he'd remembered all these years.

He tugged down her head, capturing her lips in a deep, scorching kiss that razed all rational thought. And then he rolled over, taking her with him, managing to insert a sliver of space. "Lose the bra."

He peeled off his shirt, his eyes never leaving hers, then shed the rest of his clothes. Zoe pulled off her bra and shorts, made short work of her modest panties, and stretched out against the bedspread again.

His gaze slowly, relentlessly inched over the length of her, memorizing the shadows between her breasts, the pale, creamy skin of her thighs, the enticing dip of her waist. And she watched him back, her eyes turning even darker, blazing a trail of heat in their wake.

His hands trembled. His nostrils flared, his blood a battering ram in his skull. "I've had a hard time keeping my hands off you," he admitted, his voice husky.

Her lips parted. More heat flashed in her eyes. "I don't want them off me."

Her words blasted through his nerves like a gunshot, propelling him to act. He climbed back on the bed, careful not to bump her tender ankle, and lowered his body to hers.

And then he kissed her again, his blood turning thick and hot, the pulse in his groin driving him mad. And she responded to him like tinder in a brushfire, her movements greedy, instinctive, feverish as she strained and writhed for his touch.

After an eternity, he lifted his head. He bracketed her face with his hands, met her dazed eyes. And he saw more than desire, more than need in those sapphire depths. He saw acceptance, approval, *trust*.

Warmth curled around his heart, like a candle flickering at ice. And he realized with sudden insight that it wasn't only Zoe's beauty that had attracted him to her so many years ago. It wasn't just her intelligence, her humor, or the amusing way she'd met his audacious dares.

It was the admiring way she'd watched him—as if he hadn't come from trash, as if he'd deserved a woman like her. As if he were worthy, noble, good.

He fingered a strand of her hair, the storm of emotions charging through him catching him off guard. Women had always desired him; he'd known that from an early age. They'd wanted a thrilling ride, sex with a man who was a little too rough, a chance to escape their sheltered lives. And he'd been happy to oblige.

But Zoe had been different from the start. She'd seen *him,* the man inside. She'd seen his dreams, his soul, all that he could be.

Small wonder that he'd fallen in love with her back then—or that he couldn't resist her now.

He brushed his thumb over her full bottom lip, his chest constricted with yearnings, his throat closing around a stab of guilt. She was wrong to admire him. He didn't deserve her trust.

And he couldn't give her what she needed forever—only the release that she craved right now.

He slanted his mouth over hers, and she yielded, burning him with her fiery heat. Their kisses turned deeper, longer, far more urgent. Her soft hands roved his body, spiking his hunger higher yet.

Their mouths still fused, he moved his hand down her belly to the sweet, hot flesh he'd ached to touch. She bucked at the intimate contact, the scent of her arousal a balm to his soul. She was wet, swollen, trembling *for him,* and he groaned against her mouth.

And then his patience snapped. He broke off the kiss, rose to his knees above her. The provocative sight ravaged what was left of his control.

Painfully engorged now, he slid his palms over her skin, the exquisite scent of her nearly doing him in. He closed his eyes, not wanting to scare her with his need. This was Zoe. She deserved better than a fast, hard ride.

But he couldn't hold back anymore. He found the condom in his wallet and rolled it on. He urged her legs apart, fitted himself to her warmth, and the hot, weeping feel of her nearly sent him over the edge.

"Coop," she begged, sounding dazed. Capturing her mouth, he kissed her again, entering her with a thrust. Claiming her. Possessing her. Her soft, mewling noises made him growl.

And emotions rushed through him, feelings beyond his control. Tenderness. A soul-deep sense of rightness. A satisfaction he hadn't felt in years.

Then pleasure deleted his thoughts, and primal urges took charge. He began to move, a slave to his body's mandate, giving himself over to need. He kissed her again and again, impatience riding him like a bull whip as she arched to meet his demands.

She shuddered and clenched around him, gave voice to a keening cry. His breathing grew hoarse. His pace quickened as he unraveled. And then he hurtled beyond control, convulsing inside her, giving her all that he could.

An eternity later, the world stopped revolving. His breath ragged, he rested his cheek against hers, waiting for his galloping heartbeat to slow. He shifted his weight to his forearms, his body still pulsing inside her, too depleted, too contented to move.

Her cheeks were flushed pink, her eyes closed, her soft lips curved into a smile. She reached up, locked her hand around his neck—holding him in place.

But he had no intention of letting her go. He gathered her closer, feeling a deep sense of possessiveness, along with the need to have her again. Once wasn't enough. He'd waited too long, had too much hunger bottled inside.

He swept her hair off her shoulder, planted kisses along her throat, and his body began to respond. "How's your ankle?"

Her eyes stayed close, her body boneless. "What ankle?"

He laughed and nipped the sensitive edge of her ear. She shivered, her lips parting, her hips writhing in answer, wringing a growl from low in his throat.

And a sudden fear intruded—that he might never get enough of Zoe, that he was in way over his head.

But then instincts took over, the demands of his body prevailing, and he didn't think for a long, long time.

Zoe awoke from a deep, dreamless sleep an hour later, her body utterly sated, still quivering from the amazing sex. Coop lay on his stomach beside her, the white sheets shoved down to his hips, his bare back layered with muscles, his breath steady in sleep. Sunlight peeked through the slit in the drapes, bathing his copper skin in a golden glow.

She skimmed her hand up his back, twined her fingers through his thick, silky hair. His sensual mouth was relaxed, his eyelashes black against his cheeks. And he looked so sexy, so blatantly masculine that her breath came out in a sigh.

Coop suited her perfectly. He knew exactly where to touch her, how to drive her crazy with lust, how to erase any desire to resist. One glance from those hungry eyes and she wanted to surrender, letting him have everything she could give, body and heart and soul.

He was great at sex—just dominant enough to excite her, yet tender and gentle, too. But she loved far more than his skill in bed. She adored everything about him—his enticing smell, his handsome face, the low rumble of his husky voice. The intelligence in his eyes, his protective streak, his courage and skill under fire.

He made her feel wanted, cherished, safe.

Sighing again, she fingered the short, stubby hairs at the nape of his neck and stroked the hard muscles ridging his back. Her heart twisted, the deep ache creeping back through her chest, the longing for all that she'd lost—Coop, love, a chance for a family and kids.

Her mind swerved back to her grandfather, and the hurt she'd held at bay came crashing back full force. Her grandfather had lied to her, manipulated her, stolen from her. Maybe she could never prove it, but what he did was morally wrong.

And she wasn't his only victim. Memories surfaced of rumors she'd once ignored, that when he'd taught at the university, he'd taken credit for his students' work. No one had dared accuse him outright, not with their grades and careers on the line. There had only been whispers, innuendos. And then he'd gone to work for the government, and the rumors had eventually died.

But they'd been true. She'd bet on that. And Coop had recognized her grandfather's weak character at once. So why hadn't she? Why had she clung to an idealized version of the man and deceived herself?

Frowning, she trailed her fingers along Coop's arm, her mind still lost in the past. And the truth kicked her right in the gut. She'd hadn't wanted to see the truth; she'd been too afraid. She'd feared that her parents might have been guilty. She'd feared that her grandfather might be a crook. And she'd feared that she wasn't exciting enough for Coop, that a quiet bookworm like her could never hold him, that he'd eventually find someone new.

And her grandfather had seen that insecurity and played right into her fears. He'd told her Coop didn't love her, that he was only amusing himself for the summer and had no intention of marrying her.

And she'd been too scared to question him closely, too worried that if her grandfather had lied about one thing, her entire world could collapse.

A profound feeling of sadness gripped her, a deep regret cramping her throat. She'd let her grandfather chase away Coop, define who she was. She'd followed his advice, his rules, seeking his approval, so careful to stay within bounds.

Coop had dared her to break out. He'd challenged her to be free. To be herself.

She snuggled closer against him, relishing the comfort and strength of his arms. She traced the contours of his dark, lean face, that wicked, sensual mouth. He was such a gorgeous man—dangerous, potent, intense. Far too appealing in every way.

And she'd forfeited him without a fight.

She'd been an utter fool.

He opened his eyes just then, and the scorching heat scrambled her pulse. "If you don't stop touching me, you're going to regret it."

She sucked in her breath, held his hot gaze. "Is that a promise?"

He rose, then pulled her beneath him in a movement so fast that she gasped. He nudged apart her thighs, his big body trapping her in place, his thick arousal sparking desire.

She wrapped her arms around his neck, her excitement building. His gaze scalded her breasts, igniting flutters of heat in her veins. He stroked her hair, framed her face with his callused hands, and she parted her lips, already on fire for his kiss.

But he stopped. And without warning, a different kind of emotion stole into his eyes—something beyond the desire, beyond the lust, something far more intimate.

Longing swelled inside her, a yearning so sharp that it hurt. But then he shuttered his eyes, masking his expression, and the moment passed.

Shaken, she struggled to rein in her wayward feelings and keep her expression light. This was an affair, a casual fling, a respite from the danger they faced. They had no future together—no matter what their past. She couldn't weave fantasies about this man.

Then he brushed his lips over hers, his kiss surprisingly gentle, inciting a rush of desire in her blood. She arched beneath him, her breasts aching, her body hungering for the rapture of his touch.

Casual? Who was she trying to fool?

Her life had exploded around her. She didn't know who she was, what her family had done, whether she'd even survive this ordeal.

But from now on, she was going to be honest. No more wishful thinking, no more fleeing the truth.

And there was one fact she couldn't deny.

She was still in love with Coop.

Chapter 11

Zoe jolted awake a short time later, her heart pounding with violent beats, an urgent feeling of danger thundering through her nerves.

She lay dead-still on the mattress, completely, excruciatingly alert, the pleasure from Coop's lovemaking erased by the smothering fear. What had awoken her so abruptly? What noise had she heard?

She sliced her gaze from the still-closed door to the sunlight glinting around the edge of the curtains, to Coop sprawled facedown beside her in the twisted sheets. Nothing stirred. Nothing seemed out of place.

So why was she suddenly so scared?

The faucet dripped in the bathroom. A semi passed by in the distance, its Jake Brakes emitting a drawn-out blast. The silence was thick, oppressive, her lungs so constricted she could barely squeeze in air.

But something had jarred her from sleep.

Suddenly, a faint scratch came from the door.

A tinny taste filled her mouth. Her palms grew slick and cold. She touched Coop's shoulder, and he lifted his head, indicating that he was awake and had heard the noise. He rolled off the bed, motioned for her to get up, and began tugging on clothes.

She sprang up, yanked on her shorts and T-shirt, stuffing her underwear into her pocket along with the flash drive. Then she grabbed the backpack with the GPS. Who was there? The FBI? The police?

The terrorists?

A queasy feeling rushing inside her, she shoved her feet into her shoes, then hunted desperately for a way to escape. But unless they could open the door to the adjoining room…

A sudden thump from outside made her mouth dry, and she whipped around in dread. The flimsy door wouldn't hold up long. One swift kick, and they'd be dead.

While Coop gathered his weapons, she rushed to the adjoining door. *Locked.* But Coop pulled a credit card from his wallet, slid it down the edge of the door, and popped it open with shocking ease.

He jerked open the door and peeked inside, then motioned for her to go through. She rushed past him—and skidded to a halt. A man lay snoring on the bed. This was going from bad to worse!

Signaling for her to wait, Coop crossed the room to the window, and edged the curtain aside to see out. But the sleeping man snorted, making her heart skip. They had to get out of here fast.

She hurried into the bathroom and eyed the window beside the sink. This room was at the end of the building, and the bathroom faced the alley on the side. But it was still only yards from their attackers, and the slightest noise would tip them off.

She gritted her teeth and pulled on the window, but she couldn't get it to budge. Frustrated, she adjusted her grip and tried again. Then Coop shouldered her aside and shoved it up with one hard thrust.

They both peered out. The side alley was empty—for now.

Coop leaned close, his breath warm on her ear. "Climb out and hide beside the Dumpster."

He laced his fingers into a stirrup, and she clung to his shoulder while he boosted her up. She scrambled over the sill and leaped to the ground, then scurried to the Dumpster to wait.

She huddled beside the metal bin, trembling with tension, the stench of garbage penetrating the heat. What now? They couldn't go back to the truck, so how could they get out of town?

Coop hoisted himself over the sill and dropped silently to the ground. He padded over and crouched beside her and slid the rifles under the Dumpster where they wouldn't be found. Then he tugged out his pistol and checked the rounds.

Her pulse still spasmodic, she watched his quick, sure hands handle the weapon, his eyes feral and dark. And a profound sense of gratitude swamped her. She was so far out of her element. What would she have done without Coop?

He pulled her head close to his and whispered into her ear. "Wait here. I'll check the front. When I signal, run to the garage—it's that boarded-up place next to the café. I'll watch our backs."

"Be careful," she whispered. He squeezed her neck in a gesture of comfort, and they both rose.

He checked the alley, then darted to the edge of the motel and peeked around the front. She waited, her gaze riveted on Coop, adrenaline pounding her nerves.

He beckoned, and she sprinted toward him. "Go!" he whispered. She rounded the motel and raced across the deserted parking lot, terrified that she'd hear shots. Coop's footsteps thudded behind her. She heaved in the broiling air. She stumbled up the small, grassy incline to the café next door and rushed past it to the garage.

Then she stopped, whirled back. Coop came up beside her, and she sagged against the wall. "Who was it? The men from the ghost town?" He nodded, and her anxiety rose. "But how—"

"Later. Let's get out of here first." He strode to the back of the deserted garage and began examining the line of junked cars. She trailed him, wishing she could help, but she had no idea how to hot-wire a car.

He stopped beside an old station wagon and climbed inside. While he fiddled with something under the dashboard, she glanced at the Dumpsters behind the café. How had those men found them so quickly? How had they known which room they were in? And where in the world could they hide now?

The station wagon rumbled to life with a belch of exhaust. "Come on," Coop called, and she hobbled around to the passenger side and got in.

She scooted across the boat-wide seat, the cracked vinyl scraping her legs. Coop released the brake and punched the accelerator, and they lurched across the deserted lot. Then they swung into the road, scraping their tail pipe on the pavement, and roared past the motel.

Zoe swiveled around and peered through the dusty rear window. "I don't see them."

But she knew the reprieve wouldn't last. Their pursuers

would discover that they'd escaped and give chase. And there was only one road crossing this part of the desert—with no good place to hide.

She turned around, still breathless, and turned her worried gaze to Coop. He frowned out the pitted windshield, his dark brows gathered in concentration, his strong hands gripping the wheel.

"How do you think they found us?" she asked.

She thought at first he wouldn't answer. He kept staring at the sun-drenched highway. Sagebrush and cactus zipped by.

"Maybe through the cell phone," he finally said. He tugged it from his front pocket and handed it to her. "They might have triangulated the signal."

"How? We haven't used it. We haven't even turned it on."

His gaze collided with hers, and the guilt she'd glimpsed earlier flashed back. "You'd better remove the battery, just in case. Take the battery out of the GPS, too."

He pulled his gaze back to the road, and doubts buzzed through her like a swarm of angry bees. Surely she'd imagined that guilt. Exhaustion and stress must have scrambled her mind.

What would he have to hide? He'd helped her, made passionate love to her, rescued her multiple times.

She removed the battery from her cell phone, determined to suppress her doubts. They were in this ordeal together. She *had* to put her faith in him.

Because the devastation would destroy her if he'd lied.

Rarely did Coop screw up so badly.

He gunned the Chevy's engine, sending the old station wagon roaring down the two-lane highway, its front end shimmying like a sidewinder crossing the sand. He'd been careless, led the terrorists straight to their motel room—and nearly gotten Zoe killed.

He grimaced in self-disgust, furious at how badly he'd failed. He should have been making plans, anticipating problems, and using his brain—instead of letting his body take charge.

This case was far more dangerous than he'd imagined. Those terrorists had military-grade equipment at their disposal, the ability to triangulate Zoe's cell phone or GPS—which meant the government could be involved.

But that didn't make sense. Since when did the government employ terrorist hit men? And why would they want to kill Zoe?

He eyed the boulders dotting the landscape, appalled at his mistakes. If he hadn't turned on her cell phone, if he'd kept his mind on protecting Zoe instead of making love…

He tightened his grip on the wheel. He'd screwed up, all right. And now they were in way over their heads.

"I can't get the battery out of the GPS," Zoe said. "I need a screwdriver to open it up."

"Then toss it out the window—but before you do, check the distance to Seco Springs."

She bent her head over the GPS, the hot wind blowing through the open window whipping her hair. "Sixty-one miles," she said a moment later. "Why? What's there?"

"Rider McKenzie. A guy I went to boot camp with." He waited until she'd flung the GPS out the window, then glanced in the rearview mirror. Heat shimmered across the desert. Blue exhaust billowed behind the car.

"Look, Zoe…" He didn't want to alarm her, but she had to know. "We're seriously outgunned here. The fact that they found us so quickly proves we can't do this alone.

And Rider has contacts everywhere. If anyone can help us solve this mess, it's him."

Fear crept into her eyes again, and he hated that he'd put it there. "You're sure we can trust him?"

"Yeah." He had no doubts about that. "I'd trust him with my life."

Zoe turned her face toward the window. Minutes ticked by, and the hot wind batted her hair. "All right. Let's go see your friend." She glanced his way, and the trust in her eyes nearly did him in.

He jerked his gaze back to the windshield, the car's belts squealing, the front end sliding all over the road. And he knew one thing. From now on, he had to stay focused. There'd be no more touching Zoe, no more hot sex.

No matter how much she made him burn.

They pulled into Rider McKenzie's driveway as the sun began to drop in the sky. Coop eyed the sprinkler flinging water on the withered front lawn, the open windows in the ranch-style stucco house. "He's home."

He turned off the engine and climbed out, his gaze sweeping the shaded street. A young woman pushed a stroller along the sidewalk. A group of teenagers played basketball several driveways down. After their panicked flight from would-be assassins, the quiet, domestic scene struck him as bizarre.

He walked with Zoe to Rider's door and rang the bell, then caught the anxiety still clouding her eyes. "Don't worry," he repeated. "We can trust this guy."

"I know." She managed a nervous smile.

Then the door swung open, and Rider loomed in the doorway, looking like a displaced surf bum with his long, baggy board shorts and flip-flops, his unkempt, sun-bleached hair. The laid-back appearance didn't fool

Coop. Rider was a world-class sniper, cool as hell under pressure. Before he'd left the military, he'd been one of their top shots.

"Hey, Coop," he said, but his gaze arrowed in on Zoe. His lazy grin widened, his interest clear in his eyes.

And Coop could guess what he was thinking. Zoe's willowy legs were bare, her breasts unbound, thanks to her rush getting dressed. Her cheeks were flushed, as if she'd just rolled out of bed. Her hair tumbled over her shoulders in messy waves.

Coop's face heated, his hands fisting at Rider's blatant admiration. And despite his vow to keep his distance, he wrapped a possessive arm over her shoulder and sent Rider a warning stare. "This is Rider," he said, his voice clipped. "Rider, Zoe."

Rider tipped his head toward Coop. *Message received.* "Glad to meet you."

"It's nice to meet you, too," Zoe said in her sex-goddess voice, and Rider's eyes gleamed even more.

He stepped back and motioned them inside. "Come on in."

Keeping his hand at the small of her back, Coop followed Zoe down the hall. They stopped in a small living room with an orange plaid sofa, knotty pine paneling, and a buck head mounted on the wall. Only the big-screen television hinted at the modern times.

"I haven't changed much in here since my grandparents died," Rider explained. "I'm not around a lot."

Coop didn't doubt it. Rider worked for a private military company now, slipping in and out of the country in the dead of night, on missions that never made the news.

"Can I get you something to drink?" Rider offered.

Coop stayed close to Zoe. "I wouldn't turn down a beer."

"Water or a soda," she said. "Whatever you've got."

"Sure. Have a seat. I'll be right back." Rider glanced at Zoe again and strolled off.

She turned toward Coop and lowered her voice. "Do you think he'd mind if I use his bathroom? I didn't have time to put on my underwear when we left. I just stuffed it into my pocket."

Coop closed his eyes, wishing she hadn't said that. Keeping his hands off her was hard enough. "It's down the hall on the left."

Unable to help it, he watched her hips swivel as she left the room. He wanted to storm down that hall, push her up against the nearest wall, and prove that she was his.

But that was ridiculous. Zoe wasn't his and never could be. He had to remember that.

Still grappling with his unruly feelings, he strode into the kitchen to find his friend. Rider pulled two bottles of beer from the refrigerator, set them on the yellow counter, and popped the tops. "So when did you get serious about a woman?"

Serious? Coop's heart stumbled at the thought. He scooped up one of the bottles and took a pull. He liked Zoe, even admired her. And he desired her physically, no doubt about that. The hours they'd spent in that motel room had only made him crave her more.

But he wasn't aiming to settle down. "It's not serious. I'm just helping her out on a case."

Rider leaned back against the counter and widened his grin. "Some assignment."

Coop's annoyance flared. "It's complicated. That's why we need your help."

Rider's expression instantly sobered. "Sure, anything you need."

Coop sipped his beer, cautioning himself not to overreact. He didn't have many close friends. Rider was one of the few. And he was solid gold.

"We're up against something big, involving the government or military, I think. I can't tell Zoe, but—"

She strolled into the kitchen just then, and he took another swallow of beer. The hair around her face was damp, as if she'd splashed water on her face, and her breasts swayed less in her bra.

It didn't help.

He handed her the can of soda, fighting another surge of possessiveness, the primitive need to stake his claim. "I was about to tell Rider what's going on. But it's better if you explain."

"All right."

They settled at the kitchen table, and Zoe told Rider about the events. Coop drank his beer as she talked, eyeing the movement of her lips, the graceful flutter of her hands, the satiny gleam of her skin.

He'd never met a woman who'd appealed to him more—in or out of bed. But a long-term relationship with Zoe would never work. She was a chemist. She worked in a lab. He was a carrier-based pilot and never stayed in one place long.

Besides, as soon as she discovered he was after her grandfather, she'd want him out of her sight.

Still, the thought of another man touching her made something go crazy inside him. He drank his beer, his gaze lingering on her long, shining hair, the mole winking erotically as she moved her lips. Her voice was like a sultry, throaty saxophone; he could close his eyes and listen to it for hours.

She finished her story, and for a long moment, no one spoke. The sprinkler swished outside the open window. The warm breeze flapped the curtains framing the sink.

"We took a photo of one of the men," Coop added. "He wasn't carrying an ID."

"It's on my cell phone." Zoe took the phone from her pocket and set it on the table.

"I'll run it through the system and see if we find a match." Rider tipped back in his chair, his body relaxed, his eyes like steel on Zoe's. "How much time until the ransom's due?"

She glanced at her watch. "Less than four hours now. The rendezvous is at midnight at the Mesquite Wildlife refuge."

"That's an hour's drive from here." Rider's gaze swiveled back to Coop's. "I'll assemble a team. I can have a couple of guys here in about an hour. You have the flash drive?"

Zoe leaned forward. "I can't let them have it. It's too dangerous."

Rider frowned back. "You have to give them something. And if they've got any brains, they'll bring a laptop to make sure it's the right one."

"I know, but—"

"Can you modify it?" Coop asked her. "And change the most sensitive parts?"

"I don't know. Some of the files are encrypted."

"I've got encryption software on my computer," Rider said. "Advanced encryption standard. If you can figure out the password, you should get in."

Zoe nodded. "I can try."

"Right this way." Rider rose, and Zoe followed him into the hall. Coop made himself stay in his seat, fighting the instinct to go with her, not wanting her out of his sight.

He was jealous. He finished off his beer, galled by that startling thought. He had no claim on Zoe. Sure they'd had sex, and he cared about her a lot. He'd even loved her once. But now…

Now he didn't know what he felt. He carried his bottle to the recycling bin, then leaned against the counter to wait. He couldn't possibly love her. She'd destroyed those feelings years ago. This was just sexual interest heightened by their ordeal.

Rider strolled back into the kitchen. "So tell me why you think the government's involved."

Grateful for the distraction, Coop pulled his mind back to the case. "We know both the FBI and Navy are looking for Zoe. That explains the Navy chopper—and why I'm here. But those men at the ghost town had military-grade equipment. And they found us too damned fast."

Rider shrugged. "They might have contacts in the cell phone industry, someone who pinged the phone, then radioed your position to them."

"I know." Logically, there were two groups after Zoe— the government operatives and those Arabic-speaking men. "Something just feels off about this."

Rider leaned against the opposite counter, his eyes betraying nothing. But Coop knew his steel-trap mind was as sharp as his shots. "Any idea why you were assigned this case?" Rider asked.

That was easy. "Penance. I disobeyed orders a few weeks back in the Persian Gulf. Three of us were doing a routine recon run. The rookie, a guy named Warner, went off course and flew into Syrian airspace, got chased by some Syrian Flankers and MiGs. Pineda—he was the other pilot—scrambled with me to get him out. We made it, but the Syrians raised a stink."

He shrugged. "As bad luck would have it, VIPs from the State Department were in the region, engaged in some high-level talks. They wanted the incident buried, and us out of sight. Pineda and Warner were 'encouraged' to go on leave. I got shipped to the desert to wait until the furor died down."

And to teach him a lesson, he'd supposed. It wasn't the first time he'd ignored the rules.

Rider stroked his chin, his expression thoughtful. "I heard about that case." Coop didn't ask how. Rider's connections ran deep. "You've been out of communications for a couple of weeks, right? So you don't know about Warner."

"The rookie? What about him?"

"He died."

Coop blinked, knocked off balance. "What? How?"

"Hit-and-run driver. He was on leave in Bahrain."

"Hell. That's tough."

"There's more." Rider's expression turned grim. "Pineda died, too. Four days ago. His jet went down in the Persian Gulf."

Coop's heartbeat faltered. Shock fisted deep in his gut. Pineda and Warner. Both pilots. Both dead. Both had flown across the Syrian desert with him.

"You think this has to do with me?" he asked, stunned. "Something to do with that mission?"

"Either that or it's a hell of a coincidence."

But why? Why kill the pilots who'd trespassed in Syrian airspace? And what did that flight have to do with Shaw and Zoe?

He shoved his hand through his hair, staggered by the news. This case was complex, far more complicated than he'd imagined—and the puzzle got worse with every hour.

But he had to figure it out. Their lives depended on it.

And they were fast running out of time.

Chapter 12

Coop strode down the narrow hallway toward the study minutes later, his mind still reeling over the pilots' deaths. Everything about this case confused him; there were too many unrelated threads—Zoe's parents, Shaw's supposed kidnapping, the flash drive containing nuclear secrets, and now his two murdered friends...

But those pieces had to connect. He refused to believe any of this was a coincidence. And he'd bet his Navy wings that Zoe's grandfather held the key.

He pushed open the door to the study. Zoe sat at Rider's desk, surrounded by computer monitors, her gaze clamped on a glowing screen. She'd switched on the desk lamp, and the golden light formed a halo in the dusk.

"Any luck?" he asked as he crossed the room.

She pulled her gaze from the computer, her frustration reflected in her eyes. "No. I still can't break the encryption."

He rested his arm along the back of her chair and leaned over her shoulder, trying to ignore the sweet scent of her hair. He had to concentrate, put his mind toward solving this case, instead of touching her. But it was hard when he wanted to toss her over his shoulder and whisk her to somewhere safe.

"See this?" She tapped on the keyboard, then pointed to the screen. "It's a subdirectory, a whole group of files I can't get into."

She flipped back to the previous screen. "I can access these, but they don't do me much good. They're mostly summaries, extracts, nothing too dangerous. My grandfather hid the crucial information in the encrypted files. And those are the ones I need to change."

Coop frowned, wishing he knew more about software encryption. "What do you need? The password?"

She nodded. "I needed one password to open the flash drive. That was easy to figure out. But he encrypted these subfiles under a different password. I've tried everything I can think of and I can't get in."

"So what are you going to do?"

"I don't know." She shifted in her seat, and her soft hair slid over his hand. "I thought about copying the unsecured files to another flash drive and giving the kidnappers that. But this flash drive has a serial number. If the kidnappers know that, and I try to give them a different one…"

They might kill Shaw. "Can you delete the encrypted files and then give them this one?"

"I think so. But even that's risky. What if they examine the flash drive before they hand over my grandfather and notice that the files are gone?"

"They'd have to know what to look for."

"Right." Her eyes turned bleak. "It all depends on how much they know. If I hand over this flash drive intact and they know the password, innocent people could die. But if I give them a modified copy, or if I delete those files and they can tell…"

She tilted her face up to his, her eyes reflecting her fear. "I know my grandfather's not a good man, but I still can't let him die."

Coop fingered his jaw, the emerging bristles scratching his palm. "Delete the files, then give them the original flash drive. I can't see that you have much choice."

"But what about my grandfather? What if the kidnappers notice that it's been changed?"

"We'll figure something out." He hoped.

Wishing he had a miracle up his sleeve, he sank into the leather armchair beside the desk. As he watched Zoe type on the keyboard, deleting the files, his mind wandered through the murky case, trying to make the pieces line up.

Who'd killed the pilots, and why? It couldn't have been done in retaliation. He and Pineda had scrambled to rescue the rookie and get him safely out of Syrian airspace, but they hadn't shot anyone down. Unless they'd unknowingly flown over something sensitive… But what? And how did that connect to Shaw?

He narrowed his thoughts on Shaw—the man who had to be at the center of this thing. Zoe was right about her grandfather; he wasn't a decent man. He'd stolen her work, tried to destroy Coop's career, could be passing nuclear secrets to an enemy group.

Coop had disliked him from the instant they'd met. The scientist had struck him as self-absorbed, pretentious, manipulative, a man bent on bullying his way through life and controlling Zoe.

Coop slouched lower in his seat, his gaze on Zoe, and without warning, the question he'd avoided for hours came zinging back. If he'd recognized Shaw's bad character, then why had he believed his lies? He should have spoken to Zoe directly when Shaw told him to leave her alone—or at least listened to her later when she'd come after him in the bar.

More disquiet swirled inside him, nudging him toward conclusions he didn't like. He shifted in his seat, tempted to ignore the question and let it go. He had enough on his mind without rehashing the past. But his gaze settled on Zoe as she worked at the keyboard, her soft lips pinched with anxiety, and he realized he couldn't keep skirting the truth.

Shaw had fired a well-aimed shot at Coop that night, hitting his weakest spot. He'd claimed Coop didn't measure up to Zoe's standards—a variation of the same negative refrain Coop had heard his entire life, feeding the resentment he carried inside.

And suddenly, he had his answer. He'd *wanted* to believe Shaw. It had given him an excuse to withdraw in anger, to accuse Zoe of being a snob. Because turning his rage on Zoe had allowed him to avoid confronting his fear—that Shaw might have been right, that he might not have been worthy of Zoe, that she deserved better than a dead-broke, thrill-seeking flyboy with nothing to offer except dreams.

His mind hurried to sidle away from that disturbing thought. But as he watched Zoe work, her brows furrowed in concentration, muttering softly as she deleted files, the cold truth caught him between the eyes. Shaw had been right. She *had* deserved more than he could give her.

She still did.

He'd come a long way since those days. He'd proved his worth, both to the Navy and himself, and carved out a good career. But even if he wanted to marry, even if Zoe would have him, what kind of life could he offer her? How could he ask this brilliant woman to sacrifice her career while he traveled around the globe?

He couldn't. It wasn't fair to her. He had to let her go.

The stark realization slammed through him like a Mack truck flattening his heart. And in its wake came crushing waves of emotions—regret that he couldn't be what she needed. Loss that he had to give her up. Fury that she would turn to another man someday, as she rightly deserved.

He eyed the long, gleaming fall of her hair, the seductive curve of her cheek, the golden cast of her skin in the lamp's low glow. And images flitted through his mind—Zoe naked, wearing nothing but that glorious hair, her sleek flesh swelling for his touch.

He shifted in the chair, wanting to touch her. But they had too little time, too much to do. Those terrorists could soon catch up.

And he still had to reveal why he was here. He had no right to suppress the truth.

But none of that quelled the raw need scorching his blood, the desperation rising inside.

She looked up then, as if sensing him watching, and her eyes fastened on his. He gazed back with brutal honesty, letting her see the hunger flaring inside.

She went still. Her lips parted, her eyes going soft with heat. "Coop?" She whispered the word like a plea, the husky sound spiking his pulse.

His body tightened, waging a furious war with his mind. This might be their last time together. They'd confront the kidnappers in a few short hours, and then Zoe would return to her world. Was it wrong to make love to her one final time?

Without breaking eye contact, he rose from his chair,

strode over, and tugged her to her feet. Her eyes turned soft and hot as he pulled her against him. Her body molded to his. Then she sighed, and the erotic sound torched his resolve.

And he knew right then that he had to have her. Here. Now. Before he had to say goodbye.

Cupping her face with his hand, he fused his mouth to hers. They had no future together. No forever. He'd soon go back to his flight squadron, and she'd return to her lab.

But he would make damned sure she remembered him when she did.

Zoe fell headlong into Coop's kiss, surrendering to the hunger that had plagued her all day. His mouth was hot, potent, perfect, making her blood sing, driving every sane thought from her mind.

She'd been craving him for hours on end now, thrilling to the pitch of his graveled voice, the heat in his pewter eyes. How he could affect her so strongly she didn't know, but a single glance from those carnal eyes made her want to strip off her clothes and give him anything he desired.

She caressed his rock-hard jaw, loving the scrape of his emerging whiskers, the delicious feel of his arousal pressed blatantly between her thighs. But they couldn't do this. They had to make plans, stay on guard against the terrorists. And they were in Rider's house, in his office. He could walk in at anytime.

She wrenched her mouth away with supreme effort. "Stop. Rider might see us."

But Coop tightened his grip on her hips, his eyes almost angry in their intensity, and she wondered if he'd refuse to let go. Then he slid his mouth down her neck, sending shivers splintering through her nerves, and she closed her eyes on a moan.

"Coop," she tried again, her head lolling back, her mind fuzzy with lust. "We really have to stop."

He worked his way back to her mouth, murmured against her lips, while his hands slid around to her breasts. "What happened to the daring girl I knew?"

She managed a breathless laugh. "I was never that daring."

He lifted his head, and his eyes scorched hers, fueling a rush of heat in her blood. "Pretty damned close."

His low words thrilled her. And she knew that it was true. She had been more daring back then—never reckless, just less inhibited. She'd let herself let go and acted on impulse, certain Coop would keep her safe.

His eyes flared even hotter. His obvious hunger fueled hers. It shocked her that she wanted to yield in this, that she wanted to forget the world, forget that Rider could walk in at any moment, and simply surrender to Coop. "I…"

Coop's hands slid under her shirt, and the warm, callused feel of them obliterated her thoughts.

And then his mouth returned to her throat. She tipped back her head, trembling from the surging desire.

"Relax," he murmured, his voice guttural. "He's gone. He went to pick up some things and make calls." His hands slid back to her breasts, his thumbs stroking her nipples into pebbled peaks. "We're alone."

Alone.

He tugged off her T-shirt and tossed it aside, then made short work of her bra. He pulled her hips even closer, securing her against his hard length. Intense pleasure streamed through her veins.

Then his mouth went to her breast, the sensation made her knees buckle. Shuddering, she plunged her hands through his hair to hold him firmly in place. The sight of

Coop's mouth on her breast, his darker skin contrasting with hers, was the most erotic thing she'd ever seen.

He licked his way up her throat to her mouth, making her too boneless to stand. His kiss deepened, one strong arm keeping her upright, while his other hand undid her shorts.

Her shorts and underpants dropped to her feet. He slipped his hand between her legs, touching her most sensitive part.

She froze, excitement rocketing through her, the sensations so electric she couldn't move. She clutched his arm in a death grip, frantic to keep his hand *right there,* while she whimpered against his mouth.

His low laugh turned into a growl. And she realized he was still fully clothed. It made her feel brazen, heightening her excitement, like a fantasy come to life.

He broke the kiss and lifted his head. The pupils in his eyes had dilated, the silver receding to rims. He dropped back into the chair, pulling her atop him, adjusting her knees so she straddled his thighs.

Her face warmed. She felt exposed, aroused, bold.

"I need to look at you," he said, his voice gruff. And for an eternity, he slid his hands over her skin, tracing the curve of her breasts, making her nipples draw even tighter, lingering on her shoulders, her belly, her hips.

His breath roughened. The skin on his cheekbones turned tight. And she watched him watch her, trusting him completely, his hunger adding to hers.

Her body burned for him, wept for him. Her breath rasped in the silent room, as if she'd run in the heat for miles.

And then he lowered his hand, touched her most sensitive part, and the orgasm slammed into her fast. She stiffened, cried out. And he pulled her head down to his, stifling her cries with his mouth, stroking her faster as she shivered and shook.

She couldn't wait anymore. Desperate, she unsnapped his jeans, her hands fumbling as she worked the zipper, easing the tight fabric apart. She freed him, took his long, hard length in her hand, then rose to her knees. "I need you," she whispered, her own voice raw. *"Now."*

He pulled her hips down, entering her so deeply that it drove the breath from her lungs. And the next orgasm began to consume her, this time harder, stronger, great riveting waves of it, rolling through her like a nuclear blast. She squeezed her eyes closed, bright lights bursting behind her eyelids, experiencing the most intense pleasure she'd ever felt.

Dozens of heartbeats later, the explosions subsided. Coop rested his forehead against hers, and she squeezed him back, still breathing in uneven gulps. She trembled, shivering as she came down from the furious rush, her emotions spinning out of control.

How could she ever let this man go? She loved him. She wanted to spend her life in his arms.

As if reading her thoughts, he cupped her head and urged her mouth down to his. The kiss was tender now, soothing, but then it morphed into something different, almost sad. He ended the kiss, gave her neck a regretful squeeze, evoking a feeling of loss.

Of course, they had to stop. She was naked. Rider would return any minute now. And they couldn't afford to waste precious hours lingering in each other's arms while the kidnappers' deadline approached.

She scooted off Coop, pulling on her shirt and shorts, while he rose and adjusted his jeans. Then his gaze connected with hers. And the guilt in his eyes filled her with a stabbing sense of dread.

And she couldn't ignore the signs anymore. Something was bothering him. Something she knew instinctively she didn't want to hear.

"Listen, Zoe…" He shoved his hand through his hair, and his gaze sidled away from hers. "I need to tell you something. About the airstrip, about why I was there."

The front door slammed. His head swiveled around. "Rider's back."

"I know." A flutter took flight in her chest. *What did he want to say?*

He turned back to her then, and his rough hands bracketed her face. He lowered his head and kissed her, tenderly this time, almost reverently, and a terrible ache wedged in her throat.

And then he broke the kiss and lifted his head, his eyes reflecting regret. "I'm sorry, Zoe."

Sorry? "For what?"

But instead of answering, he turned on his heel and left the room, his shoulders hunched in defeat.

And she watched him go, her body still trembling from his lovemaking, a horrible certainty lodged in her chest.

Because she had the feeling he'd just said goodbye.

Chapter 13

Coop's mood plunged as their plans took shape, turning his temper downright foul. He didn't want Zoe delivering the ransom. He didn't want her anywhere near those lethal men. And he didn't want her to find out why he was here.

But he couldn't stop the truth from emerging now.

"So what do you think happened while you were in Syrian airspace?" Rider asked him. The topic had shifted from the logistics of rescuing Shaw to figuring out who in the government they could trust. And Zoe had listened intently, her eyes clouding with confusion as they discussed the complex case. And he knew she was adding up details, noting discrepancies from the version he'd told her—and would soon realize that he'd lied.

His regrets building, knowing he was about to destroy Zoe's remaining illusions, he shifted his gaze to Rider again. "We must have flown over something sensitive. That's the only explanation that makes sense."

"What part of Syria?" Jared White, a big black man with a linebacker's neck, spoke up. White sat next to Alex Herrera, the other man Rider had brought onboard. Both men wore military-style survival vests and carted bags of weapons and gear. Coop knew nothing about them save their names, but if Rider trusted them, that was enough.

"We penetrated their airspace just off the coast, around the port of Latakia," he said.

Rider muted the television he'd turned on earlier, leaving the channel on news. He tossed down the remote, leaned forward in his seat. "All right. Let's run with that. Let's assume you flew over something near the port, something that *someone* wanted hushed up. You think it was nuclear?"

"It must have been." He leveled his gaze at Zoe. "They sent me to the airstrip to watch for Shaw right after that, so I'm guessing the events are linked."

She blinked. All color leached from her face. Her eyes darkened, filling with a myriad of emotions—shock, bewilderment, hurt. And then a wave of dull pink rose from her neck to her cheeks, and she jerked her head away.

Coop closed his eyes and pinched the bridge of his nose, knowing he'd messed up. He should have told her the truth once that plane crashed. By trying to spare her feelings, he'd ended up hurting her more.

And he'd hoped… He exhaled and scrubbed his face with his hand. Hell, he didn't know what he'd hoped. They had no future together, whether Zoe despised him or not. It shouldn't matter what she thought.

But it did.

His chest balled tight. Knowing nothing he could say

would change her opinion now, he focused on the other men. "If I understand Shaw's process right, you need two things to make it work—the information on that flash drive and nuclear waste.

"Let's assume that our pursuers are terrorists who want to make a bomb. And let's say they couldn't get the material locally—here in the United States—because security's too tight. It makes sense that they'd turn to the international black market. We know there's orphaned nuclear material from the former Soviet Union floating around. So if they located some waste, they could have trucked it into Syria via Turkey."

Rider leaned forward. "And from there they shipped it to the States?"

"It's a guess."

"A damned good one." Rider looked at White. "We'll need to check satellite imagery for that time period, find out which ships entered the Syrian port."

"I'm on it." White whipped out his BlackBerry and thumbed the keys. His low voice murmured as he placed a call.

"White has a contact at Buckley," Rider explained.

Coop nodded. The Colorado Air Force base was home to both the National Security Administration and the National Reconnaissance Organization, along with other intelligence groups. If images of the Syrian port existed, they'd be there.

"What about the photo we took of the guy in the ghost town?" Coop directed the question at Herrera, a tall, lean man with a ponytail. "Any idea who he is?"

"Not yet, but I should get some feedback soon."

Coop braved a glance at Zoe. She huddled on the couch, looking shell-shocked—her arms crossed, her body curled tightly inward as if to fend off a blow.

Then she turned her head, and the abject misery in her expression wrenched him apart. And a hard, hollow pit formed inside him, the truth of how badly he'd hurt her right there in her wounded eyes.

He stared down at his hands, unable to deny how thoroughly he'd screwed up. Zoe had counted on him, believed in him, and he'd betrayed that trust—just as her grandfather had.

"Check any foreign vessels that came into western U.S. ports," Rider said to Herrera, and Coop dragged his attention to them. "Then we can cross-reference the list with ships that were in Syria at the time. Assuming they made a legal stop."

Herrera's fingers flew over his laptop's keyboard. "When would the ship have arrived?"

Coop exhaled, forcing his mind back into the game. "It takes about a month to get to California from the Middle East. So within the last week."

"Assuming they landed on the west coast," Rider said.

"Yeah." They didn't know anything for sure. They might be completely off track. But they had to start somewhere.

White's phone chimed. He tugged it out. "Yeah? All right. I'll stand by." He clicked off the phone and looked up. "The satellite imagery from that day wasn't archived. He's going to keep looking, pull some strings if he has to, and call us back."

Coop frowned. "Why wouldn't they have been archived?"

The big man shrugged. "It could have been a glitch in the system. Or someone buried those images to keep them out of sight."

Coop's mind whirred over the facts. "The State Department was in the Mideast then, engaging in high-level talks. So if there was something sensitive on those images, they might have wanted them buried, at least until their talks were done. That's why they shipped me out." And it wouldn't be the first time the government had turned a blind eye to something to suit its needs. "The question is how far up the chain this goes."

"And who had the pilots killed," Rider added.

"Yeah." Coop thinned his lips. He hadn't forgotten that part. "Shaw wouldn't have that kind of clout. Someone in the government *has* to be involved."

Zoe abruptly rose and stalked off. Coop watched her head to the kitchen, her shoulders stiff, her movements jerky, and the tumult inside him grew. He couldn't leave her like this. He had to explain why he'd deceived her. She might not want to hear it, but he owed it to her to try.

He got to his feet and followed her steps. She stood at the sink, facing the window, a glass of water in hand.

He stopped several feet behind her, not nearly as close as he wanted, but knowing she'd object if he reached for her. "Zoe…"

Her spine went ramrod straight. She finished drinking the water, deliberately set the glass in the sink, then slowly turned around. Her eyes burned with anger, accusations, pain.

He felt the blow clear to his heart.

"I'd like to explain," he said.

"Explain?" Her voice rose. "Explain what? Why you lied to me? Why you made up some story about being on leave when you were investigating my grandfather all along? How can you possibly explain that?"

"I wanted to tell you the truth."

"*Right.* And that's why you kept lying, even after I told

you he'd been kidnapped. You used me, Coop. You wanted to get to him through me."

He couldn't deny it. He gripped the back of his neck. "I did a lot of things wrong. I know that. But I never wanted you to get hurt."

She made a sound of disgust.

"I mean it, Zoe. I got a signal on your cell phone near the ghost town. I would have reported you then if I hadn't cared."

"Cared?" Her voice trembled. Twin spots of color flagged her cheeks. "So what *was* the plan, then? Wait until I'd found the flash drive, then seduce me into giving it up?"

He exhaled heavily. "Come on, Zoe. You know I'd never do that."

"I don't know anything about you, except that you lied. You're just as bad as my grandfather. I can't trust either one of you."

Her bitterness whipped into him, but the vulnerability in her eyes tormented him more. He hadn't wanted to hurt her. He hadn't wanted to end things like this. Hell, he didn't want to end this at all.

"Hey, Coop," Rider called from the living room. "Come see this."

Their eyes held, her pain palpable, regrets tearing him to shreds inside. He wished he could crank back time and redo the past. He wished he could spare her this pain.

"I know you don't believe me," he finally said, the heavy ache expanding in his chest. "But I never meant to hurt you. I was only trying to keep you safe."

He turned and left the kitchen, self-loathing dragging his steps. He couldn't win with Zoe. Every time they got together, he messed things up.

"We got a match on that photo," Rider said as he drew close.

"Who is it?" Trying to summon some enthusiasm for the case, he joined the men now huddled around Herrera's laptop. Out of the corner of his eye, he saw Zoe come into the family room and plop back into her seat.

Herrera pointed to a mug shot on the monitor. "Abdul Mu'ti Halabi, a Syrian terrorist. We've been tracking him for awhile. He trained with al-Badr in Pakistan and heads an al-Qaeda splinter group called The Third Crescent. They claimed credit for that hotel bombing in the south of France last year."

Coop leaned toward the laptop, his attention snagged. "I remember." The bombing had slaughtered dozens of innocent tourists, gaining media attention throughout the world.

"He was last spotted in Morocco with Daleel Wasem and Waajid Kassab." He flipped the screen to two more photos. "Look familiar?"

Coop's blood chilled. "Yeah. They were at the ghost town—and in the alley at the motel. Any idea what they're doing here?"

"Whatever it is, it's big. They met with some high-placed al-Qaeda operatives in Rabat, then disappeared. Internet chatter's been heating up, and Intel's been scrambling like mad. The whole Western world's on high alert. And there's more." Herrera flipped back to Halabi's bio. "He studied at the University of Manchester in the United Kingdom. He majored in nuclear physics."

Which meant he could decipher the data on that flash drive.

"Wasem and Kassab both trained in Afghanistan," Herrera continued. "Wasem trained at Al Farouq. He's a computer scientist. Kassab went through Derunta and specializes in making bombs."

"That's it," Zoe said. "That has to be the target."

Coop glanced up. She stared at the television, where people marched across the muted screen, waving placards and chanting—protesting the new nuclear power station scheduled to go online in Vegas in two more days.

And suddenly, this murky case began to make sense.

"The timing's right. So is the location," he said. An enormous mushroom cloud over Sin City—in plain world view—would make one hell of an impact.

"Millions of people could die," Zoe said, horror lacing her voice. "Even the President is supposed to attend. We have to stop them."

But how? They didn't have proof of this theory, only assumptions. And they didn't know who they could trust.

"Speaking of which," Rider said, checking his watch. "We need to head out. We have less than an hour until the rendezvous time, and we need to get into place."

Coop's head jerked up. Second thoughts kicked loose inside him, a barrage of protests crowding his throat. He couldn't let Zoe drop off that ransom. He couldn't let her near that lethal group. He needed her out of the area—hell, out of the state! Even with Rider's men supplying backup, too much could go drastically wrong.

But they had to rescue Shaw before the terrorists killed him, and those men were expecting Zoe.

He watched her rise and head to the door, flanked by Rider and White. And a sense of finality merged with the dread. She might despise him; she probably never wanted to see him again. And he couldn't blame her for that. But he'd make sure this woman survived, or he would die trying.

And then he'd watch her walk out of his life.

* * *

Zoe stared out the passenger-side window at the darkened, two-lane highway, her head aching, everything inside her numb. She'd thought her grandfather's deception had hurt, but Coop's betrayal had thrust a death blow straight to her heart.

She massaged the dull pain pulsing between her brows, feeling so utterly drained, so battered by conflicting emotions that she longed to curl up into a ball and shut down. In the past few hours she'd fluctuated from ecstasy and desire to shock and disbelief. Coop had used her to get to her grandfather. She'd played the fool for a man. *Again.* And while she'd woven fantasies about Coop, thinking about true love and forever after, he hadn't been what he'd seemed.

Weary, she rolled her head to the side and slid her gaze to Coop. He'd driven the miles across the desert without speaking, the muscles of his face like concrete, staring silently out at the road.

It was just as well. She had nothing to say to him, nothing she *could* say.

Struggling to quell the wild hurt welling inside, Zoe blinked back a hot rush of tears. She refused to cry or dwell on Coop now. She had to concentrate on rescuing her grandfather and keep those terrorists from creating that bomb. She'd think about Coop and his lies when that was done.

"We're here," he announced.

He exited the highway, and she straightened, her stomach prowling with nerves. She pressed her hand to her breastbone, panic thrumming inside her as her mind whirled back to their plan.

Rider and his men would be waiting at the turnout.

Coop would park the car they'd borrowed from Herrera and get into Rider's SUV. The men would drive to the preserve and take up their positions around the farmhouse, while she waited at the turnout until the rendezvous time. Then, just before midnight, she'd head to the farmhouse alone.

Coop pulled up to Rider's SUV at the turnout. He idled the engine and set the brake. Then he looked at her, his eyes dark, the light from the dashboard illuminating the angles of his face. "Listen, Zoe…"

She held up her hand to stop him. "Let's just get this over with, all right?" She stepped out of the car and circled around to the driver's side, keeping her gaze averted as he climbed out. Then she scooted past him, slid into the driver's seat, and closed the door.

But he bent down and leaned through the open window. And his familiar scent taunted her, his nearness making her heart flip-flop like a landed fish. She tightened her fingers on the wheel, trying to force her mind off Coop and away from the wrenching hurt.

"Be careful." His rough voice rumbled through her, and she nodded, refusing to look his way.

He slapped the door with the palm of his hand and straightened, then climbed into Rider's car. A second later, they drove away.

The taillights grew smaller, the sound of the engine fainter, and then the SUV vanished in the night. A yawning sense of loneliness swept through her, and suddenly, she had the overwhelming urge to call Coop back, to pretend it was all a mistake, and launch herself into his arms.

Fool.

Hardening her heart, determined not to think about Coop, she waited at the turnout for ten torturous minutes, then drove toward the wildlife preserve. The tires drummed against the pavement. The full moon tinted the desert a ghostly gray. Far ahead on the highway she spotted a lone truck's taillights, the only sign of humanity in the empty night.

And the closer she got to the rendezvous point, the faster her pulse beat, the more her belly began to churn. She'd acted confident around the men and assured them she could carry this out, but now that she was in the desert alone…

She inhaled the cool night air, laboring to conquer the fear. She didn't need to worry. The men would protect her. Coop might have lied about everything else, but he'd rescued her multiple times. And she knew she could trust him to keep her safe.

The sign for the wildlife preserve appeared on the highway. She slowed the car and turned onto a gravel road. She hunched over the wheel, her headlight beams penetrating the gloom as she crept along.

A coyote slunk from the road into the sagebrush. She drove across a metal cattle guard, and the tires clattered in the deadly still night. Her thoughts skittered from Coop to the lethal terrorists, to that possible shipment of nuclear waste.

She still didn't believe her grandfather could be helping those terrorists. Maybe she was clinging naively to hope, but she couldn't imagine him planning a bomb. Why would he? He didn't need money, had no lofty, political ideals. He only cared about his work. And he never left the lab, never went abroad.

Unlike the Navy people she knew. In spite of their frequent transfers, they couldn't seem to travel enough, even during their vacation time. Just last month her boss at the lab, Captain Ruegg, had taken a military MAC flight to the Middle East...

The headlights flashed on the entrance to the wildlife preserve, and she began to sweat. She pulled into the empty parking lot, then drove to the one-story visitor's center at the end. She had to hike the final distance to the abandoned farmhouse on foot.

Her hands trembling, she turned off the engine. She stepped out of the car, then leaned against it, letting her eyes adjust to the night. Her hands felt numb. The cool wind thrashed her bare legs.

She patted the flash drive in her pocket, glad she'd deleted those files. But it shouldn't matter. All she had to do was walk to the farmhouse. Coop and his friends would nab those terrorists before they could do any harm.

She checked her watch. Five minutes to midnight. Steeling herself, she walked over and studied the map by the visitor's center, then started down the deserted trail. The farmhouse was less than a mile away, just beyond some low hills.

Silver moonlight coated the sagebrush. An owl hooted nearby, raising goose bumps on her skin. But she didn't have far to go. And the men were already in place, hiding around the buildings. Nothing could possibly go wrong.

Insects buzzed in the stillness. She passed a small shed, the soft dirt muffling her steps. She licked her lips, unable to swallow, so tense she couldn't think.

"Zoe."

She stopped, then glanced around, trying to hear over her thundering pulse. Who'd said that? Coop? One of the other men? She scanned the whitewashed landscape, but nothing moved in the night. Far in the distance, a coyote yipped.

She waited, but nothing more happened. Figuring she'd imagined the voice, she started walking again.

"Zoe." The voice was hoarse, but clear, and she couldn't mistake it this time.

Her grandfather. He was here!

She whipped around and scanned the sheds scattered over the hill, her heart running amok. "Grandpa, where are you?" she called softly.

And then she saw him—gesturing from beside the shed she'd passed. "Over here," he rasped, motioning for her to come.

She hurried back toward him, her head light with relief. He must have escaped his captors. She didn't have to confront the terrorists alone. She rushed toward him, limping slightly on her still-tender ankle, anxious to whisk him away.

But he shrank farther into the shadows, and a barrage of doubts slowed her steps. Why was he hiding? Were the terrorists close by? She stopped and searched the hills again, but nothing moved in the silver moonlight.

"Grandpa, come on," she said, keeping her voice low. "Let's go." She wasn't supposed to leave the path. Coop's friends had drilled that into her, insisting she stay in plain sight.

"I need your help," he called back, and she gnawed her lip. He had to be wounded. So what should she do? The longer she stood here and dithered, the more chance the terrorists would see them and shoot.

She rushed up the hill to the shed. She caught a glimpse of his face, his eyes maniacal with fear.

Something was terribly wrong.

She abruptly stopped. Her lungs closed up, sudden terror echoing through her like a primeval scream.

And then pain cleaved her skull and the world went black.

Chapter 14

"What do you mean she's not there?" Coop stared at Rider through the moonlight, his voice rising, panic ravaging his self-control. "She was on her way to the ranch house. We had her covered. How the hell did she disappear?"

Rider hitched his rifle over his shoulder and folded his arms. "Herrera heard a voice by one of the sheds. By the time he got there, she was gone."

Gone.

Dread pitched and roiled inside him, raw terror blanking his mind. Because the thought of Zoe in the hands of The Third Crescent terrorists...

He closed his eyes, unable to finish the thought, choked by a spasm of fear. This was his fault. He should have insisted on using a decoy. He shouldn't have let her out of his sight.

Because if the terrorists now had that flash drive, they didn't need her alive.

His face heating, he bunched his hands, the need to wreak violence raging inside. He wanted to rip the desert apart, murder any man who'd dared to touch Zoe.

"They won't kill her," Rider said, as if guessing his thoughts. "Not until they've checked that flash drive and made sure the formula works. We've still got time."

Time. He labored to breathe. *But how much?*

He had to find her. He couldn't just stand here. He couldn't let Zoe die.

Herrera and White strode up and spoke to Rider, and then Rider turned to him. "Let's go. White spotted their taillights. We'll get your woman back."

His woman? He opened his mouth to protest, but realized it was true. Zoe was his woman. He loved her. He always had. Now he had to save her.

And this time, he refused to fail.

Zoe dragged herself back to consciousness, an agony of pain battering her skull, the nausea so strong she wanted to retch. Her arms ached with a prickly numbness. Her teeth clacked in the bone-chilling cold.

She jerked open her eyes, her vision blurred in the shadowy darkness, and tried to move her arms—but they were tied behind her back. She strained against the binds, her shoulders wrenching from the effort, the tight cords slicing her wrists. A low light from a nearby room flashed in and out of focus, stinging her eyes.

And memories came tumbling back—Coop's betrayal, her grandfather's deception, the nuclear bomb about to explode.

She blinked rapidly to clear her fuzzy vision, trying to orient herself. She was in a cavernous, industrial-type warehouse. The building had a two-story ceiling, a loading dock still shrouded in darkness beyond an open bay door. And it was near a freeway, judging by the faint but steady drone of cars.

Gritting her teeth to keep them from chattering, she cast a glance at the light quivering down a nearby hall. At the end of the hall she could make out a blurry exit sign.

Then a low groan broke the quiet, and she rolled her head to the side. Her grandfather lay slumped against the wall several feet away, his eyes closed, his bushy white eyebrows gathered, his arms and legs bound like hers. A heavy growth of gray whiskers covered his face.

Sympathy flooded through her, followed by a quick, hot surge of rage. Injured or not, this man had lied to her, stolen from her, entangled her in a deadly mess. Even worse, because of his selfish behavior, millions of innocent people could die.

But she'd deal with his treachery later—after she got them out of here alive.

"Grandpa," she whispered. "Can you hear me?"

He lolled his head sideways and opened his eyes. "Zoe?"

"Are you all right?"

"No, not really." He coughed then, a deep, bronchial bark that made her cringe. Not only did his lungs sound bad, but the noise would alert whoever was down that hall.

He wheezed again, then flashed her a scowl. "Why did you come? I wanted you to keep the flash drive safe."

The flash drive. Did she still have it? She twisted her bound hands, but couldn't reach the pocket of her shorts. She rolled to her side, squirmed and writhed on the floor, ignoring the scrape of cold concrete. She finally managed to finger the pocket's seam.

The flash drive was gone.

Horrified, she collapsed against the frigid concrete, appalled at what she'd done. But she forced back the dizzying panic and tried to stay calm. She'd deleted the most critical files. Without them, the terrorists couldn't make that bomb. She just had to figure out how to escape before they realized what she'd done.

She rolled and wriggled over to her grandfather, then managed to sit back up. "Did you make a copy of the flash drive?"

His eyes turned sharp. "Don't tell me you lost it."

She scowled back, refusing to feel any guilt. She'd suffered enough in this ordeal. "You're the one who dragged me into this mess."

"But you don't understand—"

"Then explain it to me, Grandpa." Her own temper flared and, suddenly, she'd had enough. "What's going on here? How did you get mixed up with terrorists? And why did you steal my work?"

"I didn't—"

"You did. You can't deny it. I saw the files on that flash drive."

He jutted his chin, shifted his gaze. "It's a long story."

She'd bet. She shot him a level stare. "We seem to have time." At least until she got the blasted ropes off. She twisted her hands, ignoring the furious sting to her wrists, and struggled to reach the knots.

Her grandfather didn't speak, and that made her angrier yet. "I'm waiting," she told him, her patience shot. "And I want the truth—all of it. Starting with why my parents died."

His scowl deepened, giving his face a mulish look. "That wasn't supposed to happen. None of this was."

"Then why did it?"

"Because I was being blackmailed."

She scoffed at that. "Blackmailed for what?"

His eyes shifted away. "I was desperate. I...borrowed your mother's work."

"Borrowed? You mean you stole it, the same way you stole mine."

He wheezed, setting off another round of coughs, then finally caught his breath. "I had to. My job was on the line. I hadn't had a breakthrough in years. They were going to fire me and terminate my project. I'd worked too hard... and I knew I'd eventually succeed."

"So you committed a crime." And he had the nerve to claim that this wasn't his fault?

"I had to," he repeated. "No one else would fund the project, and I couldn't let it go. But then Peter Ruegg found out what I'd done and blackmailed me."

Peter Ruegg. The Navy captain who ran the lab. And suddenly, everything clicked. "He's the traitor." Of course he was. Ruegg had high-placed Navy contacts. He traveled the world. He'd even gone gambling in Dubai a few weeks back.

And he'd had the gall to throw suspicion on *her*—ruining her professional reputation, putting her at risk of arrest—while he betrayed his country by selling that work.

Her grandfather slumped against the wall. "He was a junior officer back then, but he had connections, and he was working his way up in rank. So we struck a deal—his silence about what I'd done in exchange for data he could sell. He liked to gamble, you see, and he had debts. But believe me, your parents weren't supposed to die."

Believe him? After all his lies? She banked down

another hot spurt of anger, forcing her voice to stay low. "So what happened?"

"Your mother found out that I'd taken her work. She threatened to turn me in and report Ruegg."

Zoe blinked. Understanding dawned. The arguments between her parents she'd overheard.

"We couldn't risk letting them talk," he added.

Her heart shriveled, and any lingering hopes she'd harbored about her grandfather died. "So you murdered them."

"No, of course I didn't kill them. It was Ruegg. Or someone he hired. I don't know. But I couldn't tell the police what I knew. Ruegg would have hurt you if I'd talked."

"And you would have lost your job."

He gave her the same stern look he'd always used to keep her in line. "I didn't have a choice, Zoe. If I'd lost my position, I couldn't have continued my research. I couldn't get funding in a private lab."

She gaped at him. "And that meant so much?"

"Of course." He looked as if she'd lost her mind. "Besides, I controlled what data I passed to Ruegg. I didn't compromise security much."

"Much." Hysteria bubbled inside her. He'd endangered innocent lives, helped her parents' murderer go free—all for glory, ambition, fame. And to think she'd defended him all those years.

Sickened at what a fool she'd been, she caught hold of the knot in the ropes and tugged, renewing her efforts to get free. But her fingers slipped, turned slick by her bleeding wrists. She wiped her fingers on her shorts and tried again.

But as she battled the stubborn knots, another question popped into her mind. "How did you expect to get famous in a government lab? You don't own the work. And it's classified. They'll never publish it."

"Ruegg promised to publish it overseas."

She jerked up her head. "But that's treason. They'd arrest you."

"Not in Brazil. I was going to take asylum there."

He'd had it all planned out. She stared at the man she'd once revered, feeling as if her world had flipped upside down. "And it doesn't bother you that those terrorists are going to build a bomb and take millions of innocent lives?"

"You know I don't meddle in political causes. And what they do with the process..." He shrugged. "What matters is my contribution to science, the work."

She felt sick. Her grandfather was nothing like she'd once thought. He was self-centered, dishonest, unfeeling. "So why aren't you in Brazil?"

Beneath his whiskers, his lips curled. "Ruegg tried to renege on the deal. I overheard him talking and realized he wasn't going to do his part. He was going to take the money and flee the country himself. So I wiped the computer at work and hid the flash drive.

"But then Ruegg's people—the people he was selling the information to—kidnapped me." Bitterness tinged his voice. "And here we are."

She shook her head, still stunned. His confession so altered her impression of him that she could hardly process it all. But she knew one thing. If they survived this ordeal, their relationship would forever be changed.

Not *if*, but *when* they survived. She wasn't surrendering without a fight.

She scanned the still-dark room, determined to sever her binds. Then a metal strap on a stack of nearby pallets caught her eye. If it was sharp enough, she could use it to cut the cords. She scooted across the cold floor toward it, the rough surface scraping her thighs.

And she realized something else. After her parents had died, she'd feared losing the people she loved. And now those fears had materialized. She'd lost everyone—her parents, her grandfather, Coop...

She positioned herself against the metal strap, her emotions in turmoil at the thought of Coop. But she pushed his betrayal to the back of her mind, adjusted the angle of her wrists, and began to saw.

"What about Coop?" she gritted out. "Why did you drive him away?"

Her grandfather blinked. "Who?"

She huffed out a breath. He didn't remember the name of the man whose life he'd destroyed? "Cooper Kennedy. The pilot? The one whose appointment to the Academy you got revoked?"

"Oh, him." His eyes cleared. "He was nothing."

"Nothing?" Her voice rose. "How can you say that? He was wonderful. I loved him."

"He was beneath you. You deserved someone better than him. I couldn't let you waste your life following a flyboy around."

"That was my decision to make, my happiness you ruined. You had no right to interfere."

But then she understood. Even in this, he'd thought of himself. "You didn't care what was best for me, did you? You wanted me to take my mother's place so you could use my work."

"You showed promise. I thought you could help. And you wanted to work in a lab."

Maybe she had. He'd certainly pressured her to go that route. But without his influence, who knew what she might have done?

No, that wasn't true. She knew exactly what she would have done. She would have still become a chemist, but she also would have married Coop—and spent night after glorious night in his arms. She would have been happy, accepted, loved.

And suddenly, she felt exhausted, depleted, the knowledge of all she'd lost making her want to cry. She closed her eyes, a terrible fullness blocking her throat, horrified at the injustice her grandfather had done. His selfishness and ambition had killed her parents, hurt her, and nearly ruined Coop...

She lifted her head and looked him straight in the eye. "Well, I've got bad news for you, Grandpa. You're never going to get credit for that work. I deleted the files."

"You what?" His eyes bulged. His mouth opened and closed like a gasping fish. "You erased my life's work?"

"Not quite." A deep, male voice came out of the darkness, and Zoe's heart slammed to a stop. A man came into view from the direction of the hallway. He was in his thirties, had a darkly handsome face—a face she'd seen before.

Abdul Mu'ti Halabi. The man from the stable. The leader of The Third Crescent terrorist group.

Icy frissons of terror gripped her. She leaned back, hiding her hands, so he wouldn't notice the half-sawed ropes. The terrorist drew closer, and she recoiled, the shocking depravity in his eyes making her stomach heave.

His flat, malevolent eyes bored into hers. "What did you think? That we would not understand computers?" His words were lightly accented, his tone mocking. "It is simple to retrieve deleted files. And your grandfather was happy to give us the password. Is that not right,

Dr. Shaw?" He whipped out a cigarette lighter and flipped it on, the bright flame illuminating his sinister eyes.

Her grandfather huddled closer against the wall. His desperate, high-pitched whimpers filled the air. The terrorist started to laugh, a low chuckle that crawled through her nerves.

Zoe struggled not to let her voice shake, not wanting him to see her fear. "You'll never get away with this."

"But we will. In twenty-eight hours that nuclear plant will explode. Your president will die." He flicked off the lighter, his eyes fevered. "The Third Crescent will triumph. And the world will stand in awe."

He pivoted on his heel and strode back in the direction of the fluorescent light. She lowered her face to her knees, her head light, sheer terror filling her cells. Her grandfather had given them the password. She'd failed to destroy those files. If the terrorists had nuclear waste—as Coop believed—they could easily build that bomb.

And no one could stop them. No one knew where they were. She had to escape, sound the alarm—but how?

She shivered violently, then dragged her scattered wits together, knowing this was all up to her. She sawed at the ropes even harder, refusing to let herself fail.

And as she worked, memories flitted through her mind—Coop's kiss, his husky voice, the exciting feel of his arms...

Had she really grown less bold over the years?

She frowned, thinking that over as she sawed away. Before her parents had died, she'd been a typical kid—confident, secure, happy with her small-town life. Their deaths had destroyed her world, demonstrating how fragile life—and a reputation—could be.

Then Coop had abandoned her, too—or so she'd believed. That loss had shaken her deeply, robbing her of something vital, making her fear she could lose even more. And she'd changed after that—maybe not consciously— but she'd taken fewer risks, spoken out less, worried she might drive people away.

Especially her grandfather. She couldn't bear to jeopardize her relationship with the only family member she still had.

She eyed the old man curled against the wall, and sympathy merged with disgust. He was old and ill, pathetic. But he'd also used her for years.

That time was gone.

She wasn't the same, confused woman who'd started this journey. She'd grown wiser, stronger. And no one would dictate to her again—not her grandfather, not Coop, not those depraved Third Crescent men.

The ropes gave slightly, fueling her hopes. She wiped her bloody hands on her shorts again, her resolve hardening to steel.

She refused to sit here and cower. She'd escaped those terrorists at the airstrip. She'd gotten away from them at the ghost town and later at the motel.

And now she would do it again.

By the time Zoe severed the ropes, dawn filtered through the dusty windows high in the warehouse walls. She pulled her arms from behind her back, gasping at the pain stabbing her shoulders, her wrists bloody and raw. She wiped her slippery palms on her shorts, not bothering to remove the ropes, aware that she didn't have time.

She rubbed her arms briskly to restore her circulation, then reached for the binds on her feet. Her grandfather had fallen asleep again, and his rough snores filled the air.

Blood trickled down her wrists. The darned rope slid

from her grip. She blotted her fingers and tried again. The knot loosened, slid apart.

She was free.

She closed her eyes, sent up a prayer of thanks, then stumbled to her feet. She swayed as a wave of dizziness hit her, turning the edges of her vision gray. She waited, impatient for the lightheadedness to pass, and a new worry popped into her head. What should she do about her grandfather? She couldn't leave him here. But could she risk taking the time to help him escape?

She grimaced, not happy with either option. He deserved to go to jail. He'd betrayed his country, had shown no remorse for his crimes. But she couldn't leave him here to die.

Hoping she wouldn't regret it, she rushed to his side and tugged on the big knots securing his feet. After several nerve-racking moments, they came loose, and she started in on his arms.

"Grandpa, wake up," she whispered. She ran a nervous gaze around the warehouse. So far, no one had heard her. "Wake up," she said again.

He groaned, opened his eyes. "Shh.... Quiet," she urged him. "We can't alert the men." She worked the knot on his wrist loose and pulled the rope apart. "Let's go."

She grabbed his arm and helped him stand, waiting while the circulation returned to his legs. But then he wheezed, started hacking, and her heart took a precipitous dive. But he stifled the cough, got himself under control.

And she glanced around the room. Someone had closed the big, bay door during the night, shrinking her options. She either had to roll back the noisy metal door or sneak down the hallway past the offices—and risk running into those men.

Motioning for her grandfather to follow, she rushed across the cargo bay to the metal door. She gripped the handle and pulled.

It didn't budge. She gritted her teeth and yanked harder, but she still couldn't get it to move. No wonder the terrorists hadn't posted a guard. The only way out was down that hall.

Her nerves thrumming, she started toward the hallway, beckoning again for her grandfather to come. But he wobbled on his feet, his face sheet-white, and she leaped back and grabbed his arm.

"Are you all right?" she whispered.

He nodded and wiped his sweating face on his sleeve. Doubtful he could make it, but unwilling to leave him behind, she led him across the room. When they reached the wall by the hallway, she propped him against it and paused.

She peeked around the corner into the corridor. There were three large rooms off the hallway, all with their doors ajar. Past them was the exit—fifty feet away.

"Be quiet," she warned her grandfather. "And stay with me."

She tiptoed to the nearest office and peered through the window facing the hall. There were boxes on the floor, a desk, a jumble of office equipment—but no men. Relieved, she signaled to her grandfather to follow and hurried past.

The lights were on in the second room. She pressed herself against the wall, the frayed ropes dangling from her wrists, then inched to the window and glanced inside. Another desk, a printer, and a computer—with the screen turned on. But there was still no sign of the men.

They had to be in the last room.

Her heart pounding clear to her backbone, she inched

toward the final office. She flattened herself to the wall and caught the low murmur of voices, too terrified to breathe.

The men were in there. She had to crawl past them to get to the exit. She couldn't make the slightest noise.

She forced herself to lean toward the window and braved a peek inside. Four men stood in a makeshift laboratory. Two of them huddled around a lead-plated vat connected to a series of tanks. The third was kneading a white, dough-like substance near a fifty-five gallon drum.

C-4. The plastic explosive that would detonate the bomb.

She swallowed hard, her knees shaking wildly, and shifted her gaze to the last person in the room. *Captain Ruegg.* He stood apart from the others, staring at a black box attached to the tanks, a panicked look on his face.

He had good reason to worry. His hands and feet were bound. And if the terrorists didn't kill him, the nuclear contamination would.

Zoe pinched her lip with her fingers, wondering frantically what to do. She hated to leave Ruegg there, but what choice did she have? She could never get him out alone.

And at the moment, the men weren't looking toward the doorway. This was her only chance to sneak past. She could escape the warehouse, then call the police to rescue Ruegg.

She glanced over her shoulder to signal her grand-father—but he was gone.

She blinked, stunned. Incredulity turned into outrage as she realized what he'd done. He'd gone back to search for his flash drive. And if they didn't leave now, they would die.

Swearing silently, she glanced at the exit—only a few

feet away! But she couldn't abandon her grandfather, even if *he* only cared about himself.

Furious that he'd taken such a foolish risk, she back-tracked to the middle room. As she'd expected, he was riffling through the papers around the computer, searching for the flash drive containing his work.

Disgusted, she stalked over and grabbed his arm. "Grandpa, come on. We don't have time. We've got to get out of here now."

He coughed, wheezed for air. "I can't leave without the flash drive."

"You have to!" He coughed again, deep, wrenching spasms, and her urgency reached a fever pitch. "If we don't go now they're going to find us here."

But he jerked his arm from her grasp and dug through the papers again. Her desperation surged. Her instincts shrieked at her to go.

Then a sudden click came from the door.

Her heart went dead still. The small hairs bristled on her neck. Wild with dread, she slowly turned around.

And looked straight down the barrel of a gun.

Chapter 15

"There it is," Rider announced.

"Where?" Peering through the bug-stained windshield at the abandoned warehouse, Coop scooted forward in his seat.

"By the Dumpster. In the back."

Coop transferred his gaze to the spray-painted Dumpster and caught sight of the kidnappers' SUV. "I see it."

And it was about time. He'd felt crazed knowing those terrorists had Zoe. If they hadn't gotten a break and spotted the kidnappers' taillights….

He crushed that unnerving thought. Thank God they *had* noticed those taillights. With their own lights off, they'd tracked the SUV across the desert to this blighted industrial complex a few miles north of Las Vegas—and then the SUV had disappeared. They'd frantically scoured the abandoned buildings, Coop's agitation mounting as the

hours ground on. And as darkness gave way to dawn—
with still no sign of Zoe—he'd nearly gone insane.

But they'd found the SUV. And now he intended to
rescue Zoe—before anything else went wrong.

Barely able to hold on to his patience, he drummed
his fingers on the leather seat while Rider parked beside
a chain-link fence. Then Coop leaped out, threw on the
bulletproof vest Rider had provided, and checked the
rounds in his gun. The sun was creeping higher in the sky
now, the cool air already carrying the promise of heat.

They'd better not be too late.

He bunched his jaw, steeling himself against the
mushrooming panic, knowing he had to stay calm.
Charging in half-cocked could get her killed.

But it was torture to wait.

"What's the status on the police?" he asked.

White buckled his vest. "The SWAT team's on its way.
Everyone else is standing by."

"Good." Rider closed the tailgate. "Then we'll wait for
backup. I'll watch the front. White and Herrera will take
the sides. Coop, you're in the back." Rider caught his gaze.
"And no one goes in alone. We can't afford to screw this
up. If you move, notify White. He'll radio our positions
to the police."

Coop grunted. Even with adrenaline coursing through
his veins, even with the need to see Zoe chipping away
at his control, he knew Rider's plan made sense. White
had alerted the FBI, Homeland Security, and every other
law-enforcement agency in Clark County. In a few more
minutes this place would be swarming with help.

The men fanned out. His pulse accelerating, Coop hiked
along the perimeter fence line to a railroad embankment
behind the cargo bay. Using the small rise as a vantage

point, he flattened himself to the ground, lying prone in the dirt and weeds.

The terrorists had covered their tracks well. The warehouse appeared deserted, except for that SUV. He scanned the empty loading bay, the high, broken windows along the sides of the building, the gang tags spray-painted on the concrete block walls. Beside the bay, there was a metal door topped by a faded Shipping Office sign.

Battling the urge to barge inside and grab Zoe, he surveyed the surrounding terrain. The freeway bordered the industrial park on one side. The nuclear power plant lay at the opposite end, its containment domes jutting into the sky. In the distance, the skyscrapers of Las Vegas framed the horizon, blurred by the usual brown haze.

He swiveled his gaze back to the warehouse. The terrorists had chosen a good location to build their bomb, he had to admit. They wouldn't have to transport it far.

In fact, they'd planned this entire operation well.

Herrera had accessed the shipping records for the port of Los Angeles while they'd been tailing the SUV. Several ships had offloaded cargo bound for Las Vegas this week, none Syrian. But a Cypriot flagged ship, the *Aegean Alliance,* had also stopped in Los Angeles. And its log showed it had picked up cargo in Latakia—the same day Coop had flown over the port.

Coop and his friends had connected the dots. The terrorists must have smuggled black-market nuclear waste from the former Soviet Union to Latakia, Syria, where the *Aegean Alliance* picked it up. The U.S. Department of State, aware of the transaction but involved in high-level diplomatic talks with the Syrians, had the satellite images suppressed.

Whether the terrorists had timed the transaction to

coincide with the State Department visit, Coop didn't know. Maybe they'd had a stroke of luck.

Either way, the *Aegean Alliance* had set sail problem-free, arriving in Los Angeles weeks later to off-load the nuclear waste. The terrorists had then trucked it to this warehouse in Las Vegas, where they were constructing a bomb—using Shaw's formula.

But they'd run into a couple of glitches along the way—Shaw balking and hiding the flash drive, the three Navy pilots flying over the port. They'd dealt with the first problem by kidnapping Shaw, relying on Zoe to bring them the data before they needed to set off the bomb. They'd solved the second by having the pilots killed.

Which only left one piece missing from the puzzle. The person who'd arranged to give Shaw's formula to the terrorists. The person who'd had Coop assigned to the surveillance job. The person who'd had the pilots killed to hide his role in this affair.

The person who had connections to the nuclear lab and enough power in the Navy to pull high-level strings.

Captain Ruegg.

Coop's face burned, the thought of a fellow Naval officer being the traitor ticking him off. And before this was over, he'd make sure Ruegg got his due.

But first he had to rescue Zoe.

Coop kept his gaze locked on the warehouse, his neck rigid with tension, the constant hum of freeway noise chafing his nerves. Minutes ticked by. Sweat pasted his vest to his back.

Without warning, the office door burst open. His adrenaline rising, Coop raised his weapon and took aim. But Zoe's grandfather raced through the door, his eyes panicked, his white hair billowing around his face.

A man stepped through the door behind him and

fired. Shaw fell. Coop didn't hesitate. He squeezed the trigger and took down the terrorist. Then he scrambled up, whipped out his radio. "Shaw's shot. One kidnapper's down. I'm going inside."

Not waiting for a response, he sprinted down the embankment to the building, then crouched against the wall. Breathless, his heart banging against his chest, he forced himself to listen and wait. But no one came out to investigate. Neither Shaw nor the terrorist moved.

Knowing he had to check, keeping one eye on the door, he darted over to Shaw and felt his wrist. No pulse. *Damn.* He started to rise, then noticed the flash drive clutched in Shaw's fist. He pried it loose, shoved it into his pocket, then glanced at the terrorist staring up with vacant eyes. Definitely dead.

He ran back to the side of the building, crunched through the weeds and glass to the Dumpster, and gauged the distance to the window above. He hoisted himself to top of the metal trash bin and peered through the shattered glass.

The window led to a deserted, second-story office. He used the butt of his pistol to knock out the remaining glass, then climbed into the room.

His pulse still sprinting, he crept to the door and peeked out. He was on the second floor, just above the loading docks. Stairs made of steel-bar grating led to the bottom floor.

A deep hush pulsed around him. Nothing shifted in the shadows below. Every sense attuned to his surroundings, he inched down the stairs to the cargo bay and glanced around.

The sound of approaching footsteps caught his ears.

He dove behind a stack of pallets and held his breath.

The steps grew closer, louder. He held himself dead still.

A man walked past the pallets, and Coop surged up, rammed the butt of his pistol down on his head. The man slumped, and Coop dragged him behind the pallets, out of sight.

Two kidnappers down. But how many men remained?

Keeping his steps quiet, Coop raced to the wall by the hallway, then peered at the offices leading to the side door. Still nothing. But light spilled out from the two farthest rooms.

Suddenly, a shot rang out.

A soft, feminine cry reached his ears.

Coop's heart stopped, then bolted to life. White-hot fury blazed inside him, the tenuous leash on his temper gone. No way would he let them harm Zoe.

He ran down the hall to the first office, urgency pounding like a war drum in his veins. He stopped, peeked inside, then darted to the next room and checked again. Still empty.

Only one room left.

Hardly breathing, he padded to the final doorway, then glanced inside. Captain Ruegg lay slumped on the floor, his hands and feet bound, his eyes staring blankly upward, blood pooled behind his head. *Executed point-blank.*

Coop sucked in the too-stuffy air, his hands trembling with the need to act. Because if anything had happened to Zoe…

Another muted cry shattered the silence—coming from inside the room. But he couldn't see her from where he stood.

His pistol ready, he drew in a breath to control his adrenaline and crept in.

And then he saw her—and froze. Halabi held her like a shield, his pistol trained on her temple, his forearm choking her throat. Her eyes were wild, terrified, desperate.

Coop's heart careened to a halt.

"Drop the gun," Halabi ordered.

Coop didn't comply. He ran his gaze around the make-shift laboratory—over vats and wires, semi-automatic weapons piled on the tables, oil drums bearing the yellow nuclear sign.

But no one else was in the room. It was him against Halabi.

And if Halabi won, Zoe would die.

He whipped his gaze back to Zoe, steeling himself against the savage blast of fury incinerating his restraint. He had to stay calm, do this right. He couldn't fail her now.

"I said to drop it," Halabi repeated.

"Don't do it." Zoe gasped. "He'll kill you. He'll kill everyone. You have to stop—"

"Shut up!" The terrorist jerked on her throat, making her face red, but his eyes didn't waver from Coop's. "Put the weapon down *now*."

Coop's vision hazed, tunneling in on the man who threatened Zoe. Feigning a calmness he didn't feel, he spread his hands and stooped down, as if to drop his gun. The terrorist's eyes tracked the move.

Suddenly Zoe lunged, knocking her captor's arm loose, slipping out of the line of fire. Coop took the shot.

Before Halabi even hit the ground, Coop raced to Zoe, hauled her upright, and whirled her away. He spared a glance at the dead terrorist, then continued with Zoe toward the door.

"How many men are there?" he demanded.

"Three, I think." Her voice was muffled against his chest.

He paused in the doorway and pulled out his radio. "We're coming out the back. I've got Zoe. I think we got all the men, but do a sweep."

He crushed her to him, overwhelmed with emotions, and murmured into her hair. "Come on, let's get out of here."

Not willing to break contact for even a second, he half dragged her out the side door. They stepped into the sunshine, and he blinked at the sudden crowd. An FBI helicopter thundered overhead. Police swarmed the surrounding area, along with a SWAT team and the FBI. Dozens of emergency vehicles filled the roads.

Needing privacy, he whisked her away from the building, away from the bodies near the door, away from the site of the terror and fear. Then he stopped, still holding her, and closed his eyes, unable to let her go. He'd nearly lost her. That had been too damned close. The sight of Zoe with a gun to her head would terrify him until the day he died.

"Are you all right?" he finally asked.

Squeezing his waist tighter, she nodded against his chest. "I'm so glad you came."

"Yeah." His throat thick with roiling emotions, he tucked her head against his shoulder, moisture burning behind his eyes. He never wanted to let her go.

"Coop." Her tone turned urgent, and she lifted her head. "Peter Ruegg. He was the traitor. And my grandfather—"

"He's dead, too, Zoe. I'm sorry."

She nodded, her eyes bright with tears, her full lips trembling. "He grabbed the flash drive and ran. I couldn't stop him."

"I know." Still shaking, he pulled her even closer, stroking her hair, her shoulders, her back. Paramedics ran past, carrying stretchers. Police shouted orders into their radios, and a hazmat team pulled up. The helicopter continued circling overhead, the deep reverberation from its rotors vibrating the ground. But Coop's world centered on the woman he loved, sheltering her soft, warm, *live* body, unable to loosen his hold.

After an eternity, she shuddered and raised her head. His heart heavy with emotions, he brushed her bottom lip with his thumb, wiped the streaks of tears from her cheeks.

Then a shadow flickered through her eyes, and he knew she'd remembered his lies. She lowered her arms, and her suddenly wounded eyes slid away.

"Zoe…"

"Let's not talk about it, all right? I can't think right now. I'm too exhausted. Let's—"

A man wearing an FBI T-shirt strode up and cleared his throat. "I'm sorry to interrupt, but we need to talk to you both. And, Ms. Wilkinson, they want to take you to the hospital to check you out."

She stepped farther from Coop and hugged her arms. "All right. I'll be right there." The man walked off, and she turned to Coop again. "Look, Coop, I—"

"Go ahead. I'll catch up with you later. I need to talk to Rider and make sure that we're squared away."

Her gaze stayed on his for several heartbeats. And a wealth of yearnings swirled inside him, a profound pang of longing for all that he'd lost. She nodded, turned away.

But then he remembered the flash drive. "Zoe, wait."

She hesitated, looked back. He pulled the flash drive from his pocket and held it out. "Your grandfather had it.

I'm not going to tell anyone I found it. You can do whatever you think is right."

She took the flash drive, and her voice turned soft. "Thank you, Coop. That means a lot."

He stayed rooted in place as she walked to the waiting men. And for the first time he noticed the ropes still tied on her wrists, the blood smeared on her shorts and arms.

He closed his eyes. She was so brave. And he'd failed her on every count. He'd deceived her, allowed those kidnappers near her, almost let her die.

He forced himself to turn around and stride away, his throat wedged tight with regrets, guilt and remorse wrenching his chest. She was right to despise him. She deserved a better man than him.

But it was killing him to let her go.

Getting over Zoe had been hell the first time. But that old pain paled to the agony he suffered now.

Three days after he'd last seen her, Coop raced through the desert on his rented Harley, the throttle opened full bore, the engine thundering at top speed. But no ride, no matter how fast, banished the emptiness she'd left inside.

He missed her. He couldn't stop thinking about her. She plagued his dreams and thoughts. He even suffered from erotic hallucinations. He kept hearing her throaty voice in his head, smelling her scent in the air—tempting him to track her down and plead for another chance.

But he couldn't do it. No matter how much he longed to hold her, no matter how hollow the void in his life, he had to do what was best for her—and leave her alone.

Trying not to dwell on that thought, he sped down the dusty road toward Pedro's airstrip, making the desert rush past in a blur. Maybe he couldn't have Zoe, but he had reconciled part of his past. He'd driven through his old hometown that morning—cruising the empty streets, past the run-down school, through the trailer park where he'd grown up. The town had looked the same but smaller, shabbier, far less formidable. It was just a dusty desert town with no power to hurt him now.

Time had marched on.

So, it seemed, had he.

And now he had one final visit to make before he shipped back to his unit. He neared the entrance to the airstrip and caught sight of Pedro standing beside the flight shack, wearing his familiar coveralls, his hand raised to block the sun. And a sudden warmth curled around Coop's heart. Damn, but he'd missed that man.

He downshifted, drove past the trailer to the flight shack, then killed the Harley's engine and got off.

"Well, look what the *gato* dragged in," Pedro said. His leathered face wreathed into a smile as he strode toward Coop, his callused grip strong as he clasped his hand.

"Pedro." A sudden lump lodged in his throat. "It's good to see you."

Pedro had never been tall—more wiry than big—but his body seemed frailer now, thinner, and that gave Coop a jolt. Pedro had always seemed indestructible to him, larger than life. But Pedro had to be nearing seventy, and the years had done more than whiten his hair.

"Come on in, have a *cerveza*," Pedro said. "I want to hear about that case of yours."

"And I heard they put you up in a fancy spa. What did you do all day, have facials?"

Pedro laughed, his sun-weathered face wrinkling even more. "Nah, they stuck me in a cabin in the woods, of all the damned things. I was glad to get back here to the desert where I can breathe. Although with the police crawling around and asking questions, I haven't had much peace."

Coop followed him into the trailer, shaking his head. Leave it to Pedro to prefer this desolate place. Coop had spent lonely weeks out here watching his sweat drip and he'd nearly lost his mind. He didn't know how Pedro had withstood it for years.

He slid into the faded bench seat at the tiny table as Pedro pulled out the beer. And he wondered how many times they'd sat together at this table, sharing a beer, talking about planes, while the air conditioner rattled behind them, belching out lukewarm air.

Pedro brought over the bottles, and Coop took a swallow of beer, studying the older man. Pedro's brown eyes were still sharp, but age spots darkened his hands and face now, more proof of his advancing years.

And a funny, achy feeling unfolded in his chest. It hurt to think of Pedro getting old.

"So let's hear it," Pedro prompted.

Coop nodded and filled him in, wrapping up the story on his second beer. "Sorry about the crashed plane," he added. "That dead-stick landing was rough."

Pedro waved his hand. "The government's promised to buy me a new one. I'm thinking of holding out for a Hornet like you fly."

Coop smiled, the restless need to push the limits rising inside. "They're amazing machines. The Gs they pull can blow your scalp off."

Pedro sat back, his eyes glimmering with pride. "If anyone can handle one, it's you. You're a good pilot, best I've ever seen."

Coop's heart rolled at the praise. Pedro had been his role model, a surrogate father, the only man he'd ever wanted to please. And to know that he'd made him proud... He opened his mouth to speak, but couldn't find the words.

"So what's next?" Pedro asked, steering the conversation to safer ground.

He drank his beer, collected his thoughts. "I head back to my carrier squadron in a couple of days. Navy Intelligence wants to talk to me again before I go. They're still trying to figure out if anyone besides Ruegg was involved."

"And Zoe?"

His heart thudded. "What about her?"

Pedro shrugged. "None of my business, I guess. But you always felt like a son to me."

Coop's throat crowded with emotions. He searched for the proper words, knowing they'd never come close to all he needed to say. "I never told you...I should have. I don't know what I would have done without you. You changed my life. You know that, right?"

"I know." Pedro's voice was subdued. And for a long time, neither spoke. Coop polished off his beer, grateful for this man's influence on his life.

"I almost got married once," Pedro said.

Coop raised his eyebrows. "Yeah? You never told me that."

Pedro dipped his head. "Lupe. Man, she was something. Funny, warm... But I was too busy chasing my career. I wouldn't compromise, wouldn't bend, didn't want to give anything up. My parents were farmworkers, migrants, and I was determined to make it big."

His eyes turned sharp. "I've always regretted it. That career doesn't keep me company now. I don't want you to make the same mistake."

Coop's heart squeezed. "It's not the same."

"Sure it is."

He shook his head. "Zoe deserves something different, someone better. She's brilliant. You should have seen her at work on that flash drive."

"Did you give her a choice?"

He didn't have to. He'd seen the hurt his lies had caused.

Not wanting to continue down that track, he rose, took the empty beer bottles to the sink, and picked up the flight bag he'd left behind. "Listen, Pedro. I need to go. I've got that appointment with Navy Intelligence this afternoon."

"Sure." Pedro rose and led the way outside. Coop stepped off the stoop, then squinted in the sunshine blazing off the desert floor as a turkey vulture soared silently by. And a sudden flashback to Zoe trying to take off in the Cessna made him smile.

He strapped his flight bag on the back of the Harley and straddled the bike, cranking the key to fire it up. He wouldn't bother with the helmet until he hit the paved roads.

"I'll come back to visit before I ship out," he promised.

"You do that."

They gazed at each other for a moment. A tumbleweed rolled past. The hot wind ruffled his hair. And that dull ache rose to his chest again, the feeling of loss.

"Don't make my mistake," Pedro said. "Don't be an *idiota*. Stop running away before it's too late."

Coop kicked into gear, wheeled the Harley around, pausing at the split rail fence Zoe had knocked down. He glanced back at Pedro. The old man lifted his hand, his sun-beaten figure framed by miles of sand.

Knowing Pedro would expect him to do something rebellious for old-time's sake, he roared out of the airstrip, pulling a wheelie, then hurtled down the dusty road. Damn, he loved that man.

But as the miles flew by and Pedro's words sank in, his smile disappeared. Was Pedro right? Was he still running away from the past?

The viselike pressure in his chest increased. He forced his mind back to that run-down town, the power it had once wielded over his life, and the desperate need he'd had to escape.

Flying had filled that need, given him a way to flee the pain and forget the misery of his life.

He'd put most of that past behind him, but maybe Pedro was right. Maybe he hadn't gotten rid of it all. Maybe he was still running, still avoiding getting hurt, still trying to escape a threat that didn't exist. Like a hamster in a wheel, he was spinning around and around, trapped in the pain of the past.

And maybe it was time to find his way out.

Chapter 16

Five days had straggled past since she'd seen Coop, and Zoe could no longer ignore the truth. She missed him. Desperately. More than she could have dreamed.

She tossed the day's mail on the mountain of letters on her kitchen table, and officially gave up the charade. She didn't care about the mail. She didn't care about finding another job. She didn't care about much of anything these days except seeing Coop. It didn't matter that she had a right to feel angry, or that he'd injured her pride. She just wanted him back.

He *had* hurt her. She couldn't deny that. But she'd done some heavy-duty soul searching during the past few days and made herself face some harsh facts. And truth number one was that no matter what he'd done, she wanted him in her life.

Abandoning the unopened envelopes, she left the kitchen, crossed the sunny living room to the window, and peered out. There was a small park on this side of the building, and she watched a group of mothers chatting, children playing and riding their bikes, a toddler running through a sprinkler swishing over the grass.

The corner of her mouth slid up. It was such a normal summer scene—ironic given how her life had fallen apart. But the changes hadn't all been bad.

Because she'd realized something else during those sleepless nights. For years she'd suffered the fear that her world might collapse—that she might lose her grandfather, that she might discover that her parents had been traitors, that she might end up alone. The fear hadn't been conscious, but she'd felt it pressing on her mind, molding the way she'd led her life.

And now the worst had happened. Her dreaded fears had come true. She'd had all her illusions shattered. She'd lost everyone she'd loved—her parents, her grandfather, Coop.

And she'd survived.

In fact, she felt strangely liberated. Even though she was alone now, even though she frantically missed Coop, an enormous burden had been lifted from her mind. She had faced down her fears and won.

Well, almost. She lowered herself to her sofa, rested her head against the cushions, and let out a sigh. She still had some issues to work through—the recurrent nightmares about those terrorists, the horror of how close they'd come to making that bomb, her conflicted feelings about her grandfather…

Whenever she thought of her grandfather, her emotions bounced from fury to pity to pain. What angered her most wasn't that he'd stolen her work and committed crimes, but that he'd covered up her parents' murder and blackened their names. And he'd let her shoulder that stigma for years, knowing that the charges were false.

Still, she'd loved him once, and it was hard to turn that feeling off. And while she doubted she'd ever forgive him, she hoped she'd eventually find a measure of peace.

Which brought her back to Coop.

She closed her eyes, the yearning for him aching inside. Because to be honest, she couldn't blame him anymore. Sure, he could have told her the truth about his mission earlier, but she could understand why he'd lied. At first he didn't know if he could trust her. He'd had his beloved career on the line. And later...

Frankly, when push came to shove, he'd helped her. Repeatedly. He'd risked his life again and again to save hers. What more could she possibly ask?

She loved him. She'd adored him eight years ago and was even crazier about him now. And no matter what she decided to do with her life, she wanted to share it with him.

But she would have to make the first move. She'd pushed him away and refused to talk—just as he once had done to her. So it was up to her to get him back.

She pressed her hand to her abdomen, a bundle of nerves breaking loose at the thought of baring her soul to Coop. The old insecurities reared up, kicking off a firestorm of doubts. What if he didn't love her? What if she'd misjudged what he'd felt? What if she ended up looking like a fool?

But that was silly. She knew he loved her. She'd seen it in his eyes, felt it in his touch, even if he hadn't said the words. Eight years ago, she'd let her grandfather drive him away. She wasn't about to let her pride or insecurities ruin her chance for happiness now.

Her mind made up, she rose from the couch, tucked a

loose strand of hair into her braid, and smoothed down her freshly ironed shorts. And then she realized she had no idea where he was. But Rider would know. Or Pedro. She suspected Coop would pay the old pilot a visit before he left town.

She picked up her purse and headed toward the door, anticipation fueling her steps. But then the doorbell rang, and she groaned. Now that she'd decided to go after Coop, she couldn't bear the delay.

The bell rang again, her visitor's impatience clear. "I'm coming," she grumbled. Who could be in such a rush? She sure hoped that reporter wasn't hounding her again. She'd given her statement to the press and had nothing more to say. The government would handle the rest.

She set down her purse and peered through the security peephole. *Coop.*

She went stock-still with her eye to the peephole. Her heart made a crazy lurch. He was here. He'd come to see her. Maybe she had a chance.

She stepped back, struggling to hold on to reason. He might be here on business. He might have come to say goodbye. But her heart refused to listen to her scolding head. No matter why he'd shown up, she wasn't letting him leave until she'd asked him to stay.

She jerked open the door, and his granite eyes slammed into hers, the sensual jolt making her sway. She clung to the door, riveted by the intensity of his eyes, her mind wiped totally blank.

She stared at his slashing brows, his sexy mouth, the way the sunlight burnished his copper skin. He'd shaved, reducing his beard to an enticing shadow, and she curled her hands to keep from reaching for him.

And he gazed back at her, his expression somber, looked so virile, so sexy, so much like everything she'd ever dreamed of that she longed to hurl herself into his arms.

"Can I come in?" His husky voice rumbled through her nerves.

She shook herself free from her trance. "Yes, of course. I was just…"

Dreaming of you.

She moved away from the door. He strode past her into her apartment, his nearness stealing her breath. She shut the door and turned around, trying to get a grip on her scattered thoughts.

But his eyes held her spellbound, and she couldn't rip her gaze from his face. Her heart kept flinging itself against her chest, like a prisoner trying to break free. "Do you want—"

"You."

She blinked. "What?"

"I want you," he said, his voice gravelly. He moved in close, erasing every thought in her head, the warmth of his body sapping her strength. Then he pulled her hard against him, weakening her even more.

"I need you," he continued. "I know I lied about why I was at the airstrip. I know I screwed up and failed you again. And you probably don't want me now…"

Not want him? Only more than she wanted to breathe.

She gazed into his eyes, saw everything she'd ever need. And a profound sense of rightness filled her heart. "I love you, Coop."

He expelled his breath, swept her even closer, and his mouth slanted over hers. His kiss was tender, gentle. And any doubts that might have lingered fled. This was love—real, abiding love—the kind she could count on to last.

The kiss heated, threatened to consume them both, but he eased away before it got out of hand. He pulled her head against his shoulder, his breath sawing in her ear, and the feeling of *rightness* in her heart ballooned.

"I was just about to go find you," she admitted. "I wanted to ask you to give me a chance."

He pulled back slightly, his eyes searching hers. And then he reached into his pocket, tugged out a ring, and her heart refused to beat.

"Marry me," he rasped. "Love me forever."

"Oh, Coop." She blinked back tears. "I already do."

He swallowed, making his Adam's apple dip. "Are you sure? I can't offer you much. You deserve someone better than me."

She slipped the diamond ring on her finger, fisted her hand to hold it tight, knowing she'd found her perfect mate. "I want you, Coop. Only you. I always have."

He kissed her again, until her head spun. She never wanted to stop.

But eventually he broke the kiss. "Wait. I need to tell you. I'm transferring to the Navy base at Fallon, teaching at the flight school there. They gave me my choice of tours."

"You'll be in Nevada?"

"For now." His eyes stayed on hers. "But later on... I'll get out of the Navy if you don't want to move."

She stared at him, dumbfounded. He would give up his career for her? "But you love to fly."

He gave her a crooked smile, so honest and warm that it brought another rush of tears to her eyes. "Yeah, I love to fly, but I love you more. Flying was an escape for me, Zoe. And I don't have anything to run from anymore. But I have every reason to stay."

She couldn't speak, stunned by the sacrifice he was

willing to make. "I don't want you to quit," she whispered. "I resigned my job at the lab. There were too many ghosts there, and I couldn't go back."

He stroked her hair. "I'm sorry, Zoe."

"Don't be. I've received a lot of offers. You should see the pile of mail. I've been offered speaking engagements, teaching positions—even a place on a nuclear advisory board. That's the job I'll probably take. It might involve some travel, but I won't be tied to a lab."

"As long as you won't be around terrorists. I couldn't survive that again." His eyes darkened. His hand trembled on her cheek. "God, Zoe. When I saw that gun pointed at your head... I was so damned scared."

"I know. I have nightmares about that." She shuddered and hugged him hard. "I'm so glad you found me there."

For a moment, neither spoke. Zoe fought down the gruesome memories, hoping time would help them fade. "I've finally been cleared of all suspicion," she added. "They found records in Ruegg's home of his transactions. It was clear that I wasn't involved."

Coop nodded. "What did you do with the flash drive?"

"I drove to Lake Tahoe and tossed it in. It's buried in the silt for eternity now."

"Good."

She searched his eyes. "That means it's over, right?"

"Yeah. It's finally over."

But not their lives together. She gazed into his eyes, her heart full, drowning in love for this man. They'd suffered her grandfather's manipulations, a plane crash, terrorists trying to kill them—and they'd survived.

And their love would endure, too. She didn't have a single doubt.

She kissed him then, knowing that her happiness had just begun.

* * * * *

Harlequin offers a romance for every mood!
See below for a sneak peek from our
suspense romance line
Silhouette® Romantic Suspense.
Introducing HER HERO IN HIDING by
New York Times *bestselling author Rachel Lee.*

Kay Young returned to woozy consciousness to find that she was lying on a soft sofa beneath a heap of quilts near a cheerfully burning fire. When she tried to move, however, everything hurt, and she groaned.

At once she heard a sound, then a stranger with a hard, harsh face was squatting beside her. "Shh," he said softly. "You're safe here. I promise."

"I have to go," she said weakly, struggling against pain. "He'll find me. He can't find me."

"Easy, lady," he said quietly. "You're hurt. No one's going to find you here."

"He will," she said desperately, terror clutching at her insides. "He always finds me!"

"Easy," he said again. "There's a blizzard outside. No one's getting here tonight, not even the doctor. I know, because I tried."

"Doctor? I don't need a doctor! I've got to get away."

"There's nowhere to go tonight," he said levelly. "And if I thought you could stand, I'd take you to a window and show you."

But even as she tried once more to pull away the quilts, she remembered something else: this man had been gentle when he'd found her beside the road, even when she had kicked and clawed. He hadn't hurt her.

Terror receded just a bit. She looked at him and detected signs of true concern there.

The terror eased another notch and she let her head sag on the pillow. "He always finds me," she whispered.

"Not here. Not tonight. That much I can guarantee."

Will Kay's mysterious rescuer protect her
from her worst fears?
Find out in HER HERO IN HIDING by
New York Times *bestselling author Rachel Lee.*
Available June 2010,
only from Silhouette® Romantic Suspense.

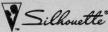

HARLEQUIN® *Romance*®

GIRLS' Weekend in VEGAS

Four friends, four dream weddings!

On a girly weekend in Las Vegas, best friends Alex, Molly,
Serena and Jayne are supposed to just have fun and forget
men, but they end up meeting their perfect matches!
Will the love they find in Vegas stay in Vegas?

Find out in this sassy, fun and wildly romantic miniseries
all about love and friendship!

Saving Cinderella! by MYRNA MACKENZIE
Available June

Vegas Pregnancy Surprise by SHIRLEY JUMP
Available July

Inconveniently Wed! by JACKIE BRAUN
Available August

Wedding Date with the Best Man
by MELISSA McCLONE
Available September

From *USA TODAY* bestselling author

LEANNE BANKS

CEO'S EXPECTANT SECRETARY

Elle Linton is hiding more than just her affair
with her boss Brock Maddox. And she's
terrifed that if their secret turns public her
mother's life may be put at risk. When she
unexpectedly becomes pregnant she's forced
to make a decision. Will she be able to save
her relationship and her mother's life?

Available June
wherever books are sold.

Always Powerful, Passionate and Provocative.

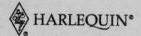

HARLEQUIN®

American ★ Romance®

The Best Man in Texas
TANYA MICHAELS

Brooke Nichols—soon to be Brooke Baker—
hates surprises. Growing up in an unstable
environment, she's happy to be putting down
roots with her safe, steady fiancé. Then she meets
his best friend, Jake McBride, a firefighter and
former soldier who's raw, unpredictable and
passionate. With his spontaneous streak and
dangerous career, Jake is everything Brooke is
trying to avoid…so why is it so hard to resist him?

**Available June
wherever books are sold.**

"LOVE, HOME & HAPPINESS"

www.eHarlequin.com

HAR75315

REQUEST YOUR FREE BOOKS!

2 FREE NOVELS PLUS 2 FREE GIFTS!

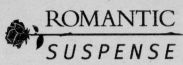

ROMANTIC SUSPENSE

Sparked by Danger, Fueled by Passion.

YES! Please send me 2 FREE Silhouette® Romantic Suspense novels and my 2 FREE gifts (gifts are worth about $10). After receiving them, if I don't wish to receive any more books, I can return the shipping statement marked "cancel." If I don't cancel, I will receive 4 brand-new novels every month and be billed just $4.24 per book in the U.S. or $4.99 per book in Canada. That's a saving of 15% off the cover price! It's quite a bargain! Shipping and handling is just 50¢ per book.* I understand that accepting the 2 free books and gifts places me under no obligation to buy anything. I can always return a shipment and cancel at any time. Even if I never buy another book from Silhouette, the two free books and gifts are mine to keep forever.

240/340 SDN E5Q4

Name _____ (PLEASE PRINT)

Address _____ Apt. #

City _____ State/Prov. _____ Zip/Postal Code

Signature (if under 18, a parent or guardian must sign)

Mail to the **Silhouette Reader Service:**

IN U.S.A.: P.O. Box 1867, Buffalo, NY 14240-1867
IN CANADA: P.O. Box 609, Fort Erie, Ontario L2A 5X3

Not valid for current subscribers to Silhouette Romantic Suspense books.

Want to try two free books from another line?
Call 1-800-873-8635 or visit www.morefreebooks.com.

* Terms and prices subject to change without notice. Prices do not include applicable taxes. N.Y. residents add applicable sales tax. Canadian residents will be charged applicable provincial taxes and GST. Offer not valid in Quebec. This offer is limited to one order per household. All orders subject to approval. Credit or debit balances in a customer's account(s) may be offset by any other outstanding balance owed by or to the customer. Please allow 4 to 6 weeks for delivery. Offer available while quantities last.

Your Privacy: Silhouette is committed to protecting your privacy. Our Privacy Policy is available online at www.eHarlequin.com or upon request from the Reader Service. From time to time we make our lists of customers available to reputable third parties who may have a product or service of interest to you. If you would prefer we not share your name and address, please check here. ☐

Help us get it right—We strive for accurate, respectful and relevant communications. To clarify or modify your communication preferences, visit us at www.ReaderService.com/consumerschoice.

SRS10R